THE GHOST OF BLACKWOOD HALL

WHEN Mrs. Putney seeks Nancy Drew's help in recovering her stolen jewelry, the search for the thieves takes the teen-age detective and her friends Bess and George to the colorful French Quarter in New Orleans. But the quest is hampered by the strange behavior of Mrs. Putney and two young women who are being victimized by so-called spirits. How can Nancy fight these unseen perpetrators of a cruel hoax? And how can she help the gullible victims when the spirits warn them not to have anything to do with Nancy?

The young sleuth's investigations lead her to a deserted old mansion haunted by a phantom organist. How Nancy uses her own ghostlike tactics to outwit the ghost of Blackwood Hall and aids the police in capturing a group of sinister racketeers will keep the reader tense with suspense.

The ghostly figure was wading deeper into the water

The Ghost
of
Blackwood Hall

BY CAROLYN KEENE

GROSSET & DUNLAP
Publishers • New York
A member of The Putnam & Grosset Group

Acknowledgement is made to Mildred Wirt Benson, who under the pen name
Carolyn Keene, wrote the original NANCY DREW books

Contents

CHAPTER I

A Mysterious Message

"IF I ever try to solve a mystery with a ghost in it, I'll use a smart cat to help me!" Nancy Drew remarked laughingly. "Cats aren't afraid of ghosts. Did you know that, Togo?"

Laying aside the book of exciting ghost stories which she had been reading, the slim, titian-haired girl reached down to pat Togo, her fox terrier. But, as if startled or annoyed by her words, he scrambled up and began to bark.

"Quiet, Togo!" ordered Hannah Gruen, the family housekeeper, from the living-room archway. "What's wrong with you?"

But Togo, hearing the sound of a car door slamming, braced his legs, cocked his head, and barked more excitedly than ever. An automobile had stopped in front of the house, and a middle-aged man was hurrying up the walk.

"It's Mr. Freeman, the jeweler," said Nancy in surprise.

A moment later the doorbell rang sharply, and Nancy hastened to open the door.

"I can't stay long," Mr. Freeman said, speaking rapidly. "I shouldn't have left the jewelry store to come here, only it's important!"

"But Dad isn't at home, Mr. Freeman."

"I came to see you, Nancy. I want you to help an old customer and friend."

The jeweler indicated the parked car. "Mrs. Putney is out there waiting. I tried to get her to talk to the police, but she refused. She won't even tell me all the details of the theft—says there's a good reason why she must keep the matter to herself."

By now, Nancy's curiosity was aroused. "Please bring Mrs. Putney in," she said. "If there is some way I can help her, I certainly will. But if she is unwilling to talk—"

"She'll tell you everything," the jeweler advised in a low voice. "You see, you're a *girl*."

"What has that got to do with it?"

"You'll find out," the jeweler said mysteriously. "Mrs. Putney is a widow. She lives alone and is considered rather odd by her neighbors. I've known her for years, however, and she's a fine woman. She needs our help."

Before Nancy could ask why she needed help, he ran back to the car. After a brief conversation, the woman emerged and the jeweler led her up the walk to the house.

"This is Mrs. Henry Putney, Nancy," Mr. Freeman introduced her, adding, "Nancy Drew is the best amateur detective in River Heights."

From her father, Carson Drew, an outstanding criminal lawyer, Nancy had inherited both courage and keen intelligence. The first case Nancy had worked on with her father was *The Secret of the Old Clock*.

Recently she had solved the mystery of *The Clue in the Old Album*. Although only eighteen years old, Nancy's ability was so well known that anyone in River Heights, who was in trouble, was likely to seek her assistance.

Stepping aside so that the caller might enter the living room, Nancy studied Mrs. Putney curiously. She was a woman well past middle age, and the black of her smartly cut dress accentuated the thinness of her body. Her expression was sad, and in the faded eyes there was a faraway look which made Nancy vaguely uneasy.

Mrs. Gruen greeted the newcomers, chatted a few moments, then tactfully withdrew. Nancy waited eagerly for the callers to reveal the purpose of their visit.

"I shouldn't have come," Mrs. Putney said, nervously twisting a handkerchief. "No one can help me, I'm sure."

"Nancy Drew can," the jeweler declared. Then from a deep pocket of his coat, he withdrew a leather case which bore traces of dried mud.

He opened the case and displayed a sizable collection of rings, necklaces, and pins. He held up a string of pearls to examine.

"Clever imitations, every one!" announced the jeweler. "When Mrs. Putney brought them to me to be cleaned, I advised her to go at once to the police."

"I can't do that," Mrs. Putney replied. "There must be no publicity."

"Suppose you tell me everything," Nancy suggested.

"You promise never to reveal what I am about to tell you?" her visitor asked anxiously.

"Of course, if that is your wish."

Mrs. Putney looked at the jeweler. "I cannot speak in your presence," she said haltingly. "I was warned never to tell any man or woman of this matter."

"That's why I brought you to a *girl detective,*" the jeweler said quickly, directing a significant glance at Nancy. "You'll be breaking no confidence in telling Nancy everything. And now I must be getting back to the store."

Bidding them good-by, he left the two together. Satisfied, Mrs. Putney began her story.

"I'm all alone now. My husband died a few months ago," she revealed. "Since then I have had strange premonitions. Shortly after my husband passed away, I had an overpowering feeling the house was to be robbed."

"Clever imitations, every one!" the jeweler announced

"And it was?" inquired Nancy.

"No, but I did a very foolish thing. I gathered all the family jewels, put the collection in this leather case, and buried it."

"Somewhere on your grounds?"

"No, in a secluded clearing in the woods about ten miles from here."

Nancy was amazed that a woman of Mrs. Putney's apparent intelligence should commit such a foolish act. However, she remained silent.

"I decided I'd been unwise, so this morning I went there and dug up the leather case," Mrs. Putney continued. "Then I took the collection to Mr. Freeman to have the pieces cleaned. The moment he saw them he said they were fake."

"Someone stole the real jewelry?"

"Yes, and substituted these copies. I prized my husband's ring above all. It breaks my heart to lose that."

"This is a case for the police," Nancy began, only to have Mrs. Putney cut her short.

"Oh, no! The police must learn nothing about what happened!"

Nancy regarded the woman intently. "Why are you so opposed to talking to anyone except me?" she asked.

"Well, I'm afraid if I call in the police there will be a lot of publicity."

"Is that your real reason, Mrs. Putney?" Nancy was certain that the widow was deliberately withholding the truth. "If I am to help you, I must know everything."

After a pause Mrs. Putney, speaking in a whisper, said, "One night, several weeks ago, my dear husband's spirit came to me. I awoke, or thought I did, and heard a far-off voice. I'm sure it was Henry's. He instructed me to bury the jewels in a place which he described in minute detail and warned me never to reveal to any man or woman that he had told me to do it. Otherwise he would never permit me to hear from him again."

"But he didn't say anything about not telling a girl?" Nancy asked.

"No. That is why I risked coming to you. I need your help desperately. Oh, I hope my coming won't spoil everything!"

Nancy, who did not believe in ghosts or spirits, nevertheless respected Mrs. Putney's belief and was diplomatic in her reply.

"I'm sure that coming to me will not spoil anything," she said. "You must have been robbed by someone who saw you hiding your jewelry, and who knew its value."

"But I told no one my plan."

"I'd like to see the place where you buried the leather case. Why don't we drive out there now in my car?"

"If you like," the widow agreed halfheartedly.

Nancy explained to Mrs. Gruen that she would be gone for an hour or so. Nancy's mother was not living. For many years, the Drew household had been efficiently run by Hannah Gruen, who had been with the family so long that she was regarded as one of them. She loved Nancy as a daughter, and worried a great deal about her whenever the young detective undertook to solve a mystery.

Taking Togo along, Nancy and Mrs. Putney drove through the countryside to the edge of a dense woods which bordered the highway. At Mrs. Putney's direction, Nancy turned down a narrow side road, crossed an old-fashioned covered bridge, and finally parked beneath an arch of thickly interlaced tree limbs.

As the two alighted, a gentle breeze rippled Nancy's hair and stirred the leaves overhead. The rustling in the branches seemed to make Togo uneasy. He pricked up his ears and began to growl.

"Quiet, Togo!" Nancy ordered. "You'd better stay in the car," she added, raising the windows part way. "You might race off into the woods."

"Follow me," Mrs. Putney directed, setting off through a path that curved among the tall trees.

The widow reached a small clearing a few hundred yards from the roadside and halted. Without speaking, she pointed to the center of a grassy place where a section of earth had been dug up.

Nancy glanced around carefully. On all sides, the clearing was shielded by a dense growth of bushes. Quickly she set about inspecting the spot where the leather case had been buried.

The ground was soft, for it had rained hard during the night. If there had been footprints other than those of Mrs. Putney, they had been washed away.

As Nancy straightened up, she heard a car pass along the road. It slowed as if the driver intended to stop, then speeded on.

Nancy continued systematically to search the area for evidence. She was about to abandon the task when her gaze fell upon a scrap of paper which had snagged at the base of a thorny bush. Picking it up, Nancy noticed that it was a page torn from a catalog. On one side was the advertisement:

"BEAUTIFUL LIGHTS, $10.00." On the other, "NO ASSISTANTS."

Doubtful as to the value of the find, Nancy nevertheless slipped the paper into her purse. As she did so, her eyes came to rest upon a long, shiny piece of metal a few feet away.

Before she could pick it up, an agonized scream cut through the silent woods!

CHAPTER II

The First Clue

NANCY whirled around and was relieved to see that Mrs. Putney was safe. The bloodcurdling scream must have come from the road.

"What was that?" The widow was trembling.

"Someone's in trouble!" Nancy exclaimed. "It was a woman's voice!"

Nancy began running in the direction of the road. Mrs. Putney followed as fast as she could.

Out of breath, Nancy reached the place where she had left her convertible. Togo was jumping from seat to seat, barking excitedly.

"Maybe you know something, old boy," Nancy said, and let him out on a leash.

She allowed him to lead her a short distance down the road. He began sniffing the ground, where Nancy noticed some fresh tire prints. Before they reached the first bend in the highway, she heard the muffled roar of a car engine.

"A car must have been parked just out of sight!" she murmured. "Now it's pulling away!"

Though she and Togo ran, the automobile had disappeared by the time they rounded the bend. The dog at this point seemed to lose interest.

"The woman who screamed must have been in the car," Nancy decided. "But who was she? And why did she scream?"

It was too late to attempt pursuit. Thoughtfully Nancy walked back to her own car, where Mrs. Putney anxiously awaited her.

"Did you learn anything, Nancy?"

"Nothing of importance. No one seems to be around here now."

"It was such a horrible scream." Mrs. Putney shivered. "Please, let's leave. I feel so uneasy here—as if unfriendly spirits were watching!"

Nancy suddenly remembered the object in the grass which had drawn her attention just before she had heard the scream. "I'd like to return to the clearing for a minute or two," she said. "Mrs. Putney, why don't you wait here in the car?"

"I believe I will," the widow agreed, quickly getting into the automobile. "But please hurry!"

"I will," Nancy promised.

She started off through the woods with Togo. Though she did not for an instant share Mrs. Putney's belief that "spirits were watching," the woods depressed her.

"I've allowed Mrs. Putney's ghost talk to get on my nerves!" Nancy chided herself.

As she approached the spot where Mrs. Putney had buried the jewelry, Togo began to act strangely. Twice he paused to sniff the air and whine. Once he looked up into Nancy's face as if trying to tell her something, and growled.

"Togo, what is it?" Nancy asked. "One would think—"

She gazed alertly about the clearing. It was deserted, yet every rustle of the leaves seemed to warn her to be careful.

Rather annoyed at her misgivings, Nancy went to the spot where she had been about to pick up the metallic object. Though she looked everywhere, the young detective was unable to find it.

Now more than ever alert, she carefully looked at the ground. In several places the grass had been trampled by herself, Mrs. Putney, or by someone else.

Togo began to sniff and tug at his leash. The dog led her to a depression in the ground which was hidden by bushes. Plainly visible in the soft earth were the prints of a man's shoes.

Stooping down, she examined the footprints thoroughly, measuring them with her hand. Obviously they were fresh. The narrowness of the shoe, and its length, led Nancy to believe that the man who had walked there was tall and thin.

"So that's why I can't find the piece of metal!"

she decided. "He came and picked it up while I was investigating the woman's scream! And probably," Nancy thought ruefully, "she was with him, and her scream was to frighten me away."

Though the trail was indistinct, Nancy could follow the footprints to the shelf of land which overlooked the clearing. The stranger had concealed himself there, watching!

"If he didn't go off in the car, he may not be far from here now," Nancy decided uneasily. "He may be the jewel thief!"

Nancy's attractive face tightened as she realized that danger might be lurking in the forest. She was convinced that the theft of Mrs. Putney's buried treasure was no ordinary affair.

"Only a very clever thief would have taken the trouble to substitute fake pieces of jewelry," she thought. "No doubt it was done to keep Mrs. Putney from discovering her loss and reporting the theft to the police."

Wasting no further time in reflection, Nancy followed the footprints. When the marks were no longer visible, Togo sniffed the ground intelligently, and led her to the road, where he stopped.

"So the man did go off in the car," she sighed.

With Togo trotting along beside her, Nancy returned to her convertible.

"I'm so glad you're back," Mrs. Putney said, greatly relieved. "I was beginning to worry."

En route to River Heights, Nancy said nothing

of her findings, except that she thought the footprints might have been made by the thief. Her companion now seemed only mildly interested, and responded absent-mindedly to questions.

When they came to the city, Mrs. Putney requested that she be dropped off at Mr. Freeman's jewelry store. Reminding her that the case of fake jewelry had been left at the Drew home, Nancy asked what should be done with it.

"I'll get it later," Mrs. Putney decided.

Nancy was pleased to have the case left in her possession, and promptly asked permission to show the jewelry to her father.

"By all means do so," Mrs. Putney said. "Only please be careful not to reveal what I told you about my husband or his instructions."

Nancy promised. After leaving the widow, she drove directly home. When her father arrived from his office, she had the collection spread out on the living-room table in front of her.

"Well, well! What's going on here?" the lawyer exclaimed, pausing to stare. "Have you been robbing jewelry stores lately, Nancy?"

Carson Drew was a tall, distinguished-looking man of middle age, with keen, twinkling blue eyes like those of his daughter. He and his only child were companionable and shared a delightful sense of humor. Nancy sprang up to hug him.

"Dad, I had the most exciting afternoon!"

"Ha! Another mystery!" the lawyer said with a mock groan.

"I think it's going to be a very interesting one. Just look at this fake jewelry!"

Mr. Drew examined the pieces one by one, while Nancy related some of the story.

"One or two facts I can't tell," she said reluctantly. "Mrs. Putney swore me to secrecy."

"I don't like that, Nancy."

"Neither do I, Dad, but in a day or so, she'll change her mind. Meanwhile, I can't pass up a good mystery!"

"I suppose not," her father replied. "The point is, if you're determined to try to help Mrs. Putney, you must be very cautious."

Mr. Drew picked up a jewel-studded pin, studied it a moment, and added, "Whoever made this is a clever craftsman. He must have plotted every move far in advance, for it takes time to make imitations like this."

"Dad, do you suppose a River Heights jeweler made these pieces?"

"Possible. However, I'm sure our jewelers are honest merchants, and if they made the imitations, they did so in good faith."

Nancy replaced the jewelry in the leather case.

"Tomorrow I'll show these pieces to a few of the River Heights stores, and perhaps someone can identify the work."

Soon after breakfast the next morning, Nancy set forth on a tour of jewelry stores. Bigelow Company was the last establishment at which she called, and there luck was with her. Mr. Bigelow, one of the owners, stated positively that the imitations had not been made by his firm, but he gave Nancy a suggestion.

"Look for a man named Howard Brex," the jeweler said. "He was a salesman and former designer for a New Orleans house. Used to sell jewelry to me. Not a bad-looking fellow—tall, dark, slender, and a smooth talker. He was a slippery character, though. Finally went to prison for fraud. Maybe he's been released."

Nancy became excited upon hearing this description of Brex. The footprints in the woods had been those of a tall, slender man!

After thanking Mr. Bigelow for the information, Nancy hurried to her father's office. Perching herself on his desk, she asked him if he had any information about Howard Brex in his files. Ringing for his secretary, the lawyer sent for a certain loose-leaf file and fingered through the B's.

"Brex was released a few months ago from a Louisiana penitentiary with time off for good behavior," Mr. Drew revealed. "You think he may be your thief?"

"Oh, I do," she replied, thrilled at the possibility that she had uncovered a real clue.

The arrival of a client cut short further conversation. Nancy telephoned Mr. Bigelow from the outer office and got the name of Brex's former employer in New Orleans. Then she started for home, a plan of action in mind.

Upon arriving at the Drew house, she was pleasantly surprised to find two friends, Bess Marvin and another girl, George Fayne, on the front porch.

George, her dark hair cut in an attractive short style, was deeply tanned. By contrast, her plump cousin Bess was blonde and fair-complexioned.

"I may have some news for you," Nancy hinted as they entered the house. She left Bess and George in the living room and went to telephone Mrs. Putney. After assuring the widow that her two assistants were girls, Nancy obtained reluctant permission to explain the circumstances of the case to Bess and George.

Rejoining the girls, Nancy said, "How would you two like to go to New Orleans with me?"

CHAPTER III

Tracking a Thief

"NEW ORLEANS!" Bess and George exclaimed.

Nancy smiled at her friends. "I'm working on a new case," she said. "Right now, I'm looking for a tall, dark man."

Bess giggled. "What would Ned say to that?"

Nancy blushed as she replied that the man she was after was probably a thief. Furthermore, the place to start looking for him was New Orleans. She told them the story, saying Brex's former employer should be able to recognize the craftsmanship in any imitation jewelry Brex might have made.

"Dad promised me a trip," Nancy said. "I know he can't go with me now. Tonight I'll ask him if you girls can take his place; that is, if you'd like to go."

"Would we!" exclaimed George.

"While we're investigating this Brex person,

George and I can do some sightseeing," remarked Bess. "New Orleans is such a romantic city!"

A twinkle came into Nancy's eyes. "I'm taking you girls along for protection," she said.

"Oh, we won't desert you." George grinned. "But all work and no play isn't any fun."

That evening Nancy discussed the plan with her father. He readily gave his consent.

Not only might a conference with Howard Brex's former employer bring results, he agreed, but there was a possibility that the suspect might even pawn the stolen articles in his home town.

"It's the most likely place for him to have a fence," declared the lawyer.

As Nancy hurried to the telephone to call her friends, he warned her to be careful in following up the clue in the distant city. To Nancy's delight, George and Bess also received permission to make the trip.

Hannah Gruen helped Nancy pack, while Mr. Drew made plane and hotel reservations. Before leaving, Nancy telephoned to Mrs. Putney to ask permission to take the imitation jewelry to New Orleans.

"I appreciate your efforts," the widow said, "but I'm sure nothing will come of the trip."

"Why do you say that, Mrs. Putney?"

"Last night I had another message from my departed husband. He said the thief who stole my jewelry lost it in a large body of water, and it'll never be recovered!"

Nancy was skeptical of the widow's messages but wisely did not argue with Mrs. Putney. She simply said she would be leaving in the morning with her two friends, and promised to report to the widow immediately upon her return.

The next day the three girls boarded the plane for New Orleans. The day was perfect for flying. An attractive hostess served them a tasty lunch and spent most of her spare time chatting with them.

Once, when the plane stopped briefly to pick up passengers, the girls alighted for a little while to stretch their legs. Upon taking their seats again, they noticed that a dark-haired woman in her late thirties had taken the empty seat next to Bess. She regarded the three intently as they sat down, and smiled in a friendly manner.

"Is this your first plane trip?" she asked Bess.

"No!" Bess replied. Then, not wishing to be rude, she added, "We're going to New Orleans."

"You'll love the city!" the woman declared. "Where are you staying?"

Bess told her. Nancy, seated in front of them, was sorry their hotel had been named. She had wanted to keep their visit to New Orleans as secret as possible. When they reached their hotel George scolded her cousin.

"You'll never learn to be a detective, Bess," she

said severely. "You can't tell who that woman on the plane might be."

Nancy, acting as peacemaker, said, "Let's forget it, girls, and do some sightseeing. It's too late to call on Mr. Johnson, Howard Brex's former boss, today. We'll go there in the morning."

Nancy's friends soon found that she did not intend to spend the time in mere sightseeing. Whenever she came to a jewelry shop, or a pawnshop that was open, she insisted that they go in and look at the jewelry on display.

The trip proved to be pleasurable, if not profitable. Their inquiries led them into many sections of New Orleans. The French Quarter, where the buildings were charming in their elegance of a bygone day, interested them most. Beautiful ironwork, delicately tinted plaster walls, old courtyards, once the center of fashionable Creole family life, fascinated the girls.

On a balcony, a bright-colored parrot chattered at them in friendly fashion. A smiling woman, bearing a basket of flowers, stopped to sell a flower to each girl. On all sides, the visitors saw interesting characters, and heard the soft-spoken dialect which was a blend of French, Cajun, and Gumbo.

Bess sighed contentedly. "If I could only spend a month in this lovely old city!" she said.

"It would be nice," Nancy agreed. "But come on. Here's another shop."

It was the fifteenth they had visited, and even Nancy was becoming weary. She had not seen any trace of the stolen jewelry.

"Let's quit," urged Bess. "I'm starved. Suppose we go to one of those famous restaurants and have oysters baked with garlic, and Creole shrimp, and—"

"And take on five pounds," scoffed George, looking with disfavor at Bess's generous weight.

But the girls ate sensibly and went to bed early. In the morning they accompanied Nancy to the jewelry firm for which Howard Brex had worked. Mr. Johnson, the head of the company, was most cooperative. He studied the imitation jewelry which Nancy showed him, and compared it to some pieces of his own which Brex had made.

"I'd certainly say that all of these were made by the same man," Mr. Johnson declared.

Then he told the girls what he knew of his former salesman. "He was a fine craftsman and made excellent designs," Mr. Johnson said. "Too bad he got into trouble."

"I understand he's been released from prison," Nancy said. "Have you any idea where he is?"

"Not the slightest, but I'll be glad to let you know if I hear anything."

Nancy left both her hotel address and that of her River Heights home. She was in a thoughtful mood as she accompanied her friends on their round of sightseeing and to lunch in a quaint restaurant.

"New Orleans is wonderful!" Bess exclaimed. Counting on her fingers, she added, "We've seen the banana wharf, the market, the garden district, and that old cemetery where all the dead are buried in tombs above the ground."

"That's because this place is below sea level," said George. "Say, do you suppose that guide thought we believed the story about the tomb which is supposed to glow at night with an unearthly light?"

"He said spirits come out and weave back and forth like wisps of fog," said Bess.

"That's just what they are—fog," George declared practically.

"Oh, I don't for a minute believe in ghosts," Bess replied quickly.

"I wish we had time to go to Grand Isle, the haunt of Lafitte and his men," said Nancy.

"Who is he?" Bess asked.

"He was a famous pirate," Nancy replied. "According to tradition, when burying treasure, he always murdered one of his band and left his ghost to guard the hidden loot!"

As the girls left the restaurant and started up the street, Nancy happened to turn around. Emerging from the door of the restaurant was a woman.

"Girls," Nancy said in a whisper, "don't look now, but the woman who was on the plane just came out of our restaurant. I think she was spying on us!"

"Why would she do that?" Bess asked.

"If she follows us, then I'll be convinced she's trying to find out what we're up to in New Orleans," Nancy replied.

To prove her point, the young sleuth turned down one street and up another. The woman did the same.

"I'm going to try something," Nancy said quietly. "Two can play this game."

It was easy for the girls to dodge into three different shops as they rounded another corner. Their pursuer, confused, stood on the sidewalk for several seconds, then turned and walked back in the direction from which she had come. Cautiously Nancy emerged, then Bess and George.

The girls trailed the woman for several blocks. Though there were many pedestrians on the street, they were able to keep their quarry in sight. Apparently she was in a hurry, for she walked quickly, not once slackening her pace. As they rounded a corner, she suddenly disappeared into an alley. Nancy darted forward, just in time to see the woman enter a building.

When she and her friends reached it, Bess was not in favor of continuing the search. Nancy insisted the place was innocent-looking enough, and walked through the open arch. In the distance the girls could hear low singing.

They proceeded down a dimly lighted hall, and in a moment the girls stood beside the door beyond which the singing was coming. A placard on it read: *Church of Eternal Harmony*.

Bess, intrigued, lost her fears and urged that they go inside. Nancy hesitated. At that moment the door opened. A man with long white hair and a beard invited them to enter.

"Our admission is reasonable," he said, smiling. "Only two dollars. If the spirit speaks, your questions will be answered."

Still Nancy hesitated. She realized now that a séance was going on inside. Having no desire to spend two dollars so foolishly, she was about to retreat, when Bess walked boldly into the room beyond. George followed, and Nancy was forced to go along.

After paying admission they seated themselves on a bench near the door. The singing had ceased, and as the girls' eyes grew accustomed to the dim lights, they could see that a number of people sat on benches scattered about the place.

On one wall hung a life-size portrait of a woman swathed in white veils up to her eyes. Long dark hair fell below her shoulders. Every face in the room was upturned, gazing at the portrait.

Presently the white-bearded man announced

that all would have to help summon her spirit.

"Let us sit around this table," he intoned.

Bess stood up to go forward, but Nancy pulled her back to the bench. Several others in the room arose and seated themselves on chairs around an oblong table. The old man took his place at the head of it, his back against the wall, a few feet beyond the portrait.

"Let no one utter a sound," he requested.

Silence fell upon the room. Nancy strained her eyes toward the table, watching intently. The white-bearded man sat perfectly still, looking straight ahead of him. Presently a smile flickered over his face.

"I feel the spirits approaching," he said in a scarcely audible voice.

The words were hardly out of his mouth when three raps were heard. The old man, looking pleased, interpreted the sounds as meaning, "I am here," and invited the participants to ask the spirit for answers to their problems. He explained that one rap would mean Yes, two No, and five would mean that danger lay ahead and the questioner should take every precaution to avoid it.

For several seconds no one spoke. The spirit gave three more sharp raps. Then, shyly, a woman at the table asked:

"Will my child be ill long?"

There came two sharp raps, and the questioner

gave a sigh of relief. Another silence followed. Nancy felt Bess lean forward. Out of the corner of her eye, Nancy had noted that her friend was completely entranced by what was going on. Realizing that Bess was about to ask a question, and fearful she might say something about Mrs. Putney's mystery, Nancy leaned over and whispered into her friend's ear:

"Please don't say anything!"

"Silence!" ordered the old man at the table. "Do you wish to drive away our friendly spirit? Ill luck follows him who disturbs the work of the spirit."

As he spoke, the dim lights faded out. The room was in complete darkness.

Suddenly, on the wall above the portrait, a faint glow appeared. It grew larger, until the whole portrait seemed to be taking form. Bess and George, seated on either side of Nancy, huddled close to her.

Bess nervously clutched her friend's arm until Nancy winced from the pressure. The next moment the three girls gasped.

The portrait had come to life!

The white-bearded man arose from his chair.

"Good people," he said, "Amurah has come to us to speak. But she will answer only the most important questions. Approach no closer, or her lifelike spirit will vanish on the wind."

"Oh, Amurah, tell me, please," implored a young woman from a far corner of the room, "if Thomas comes back to me, shall I marry him?"

Amurah lowered her eyes, then nodded.

"Oh, thank you, thank you," the young woman exclaimed, delight in her voice.

Again Nancy could feel that Bess was about to ask a question. Quietly she laid a finger across the girl's lips. The light around the portrait began to fade.

"Alas, the spirits are leaving us!" the white-bearded medium interpreted.

A few seconds later the lights came on in the room. The old man, arising, made a low bow to the portrait, then announced he regretted that the spirits had not been able to remain long enough to answer the questions of all those present.

"Should you wish further knowledge," he said, "you may seek it from Norman Towner, a photographer, who has a direct connection with the spirit world. From time to time messages appear upon Mr. Towner's photographic plates."

The man ushered his clients from the room, but not before each of them had paused to look at Amurah. George had the temerity to touch the canvas. There was no question but that it was only a portrait. Upon reaching the street, the three girls paused.

"Wasn't it wonderful!" Bess exclaimed, adding

that they should go at once to the studio of Norman Towner.

"Nonsense," George said. "You've already spent two dollars and got nothing for it."

"That's because Nancy wouldn't let me ask a question," Bess argued. "Maybe I'll get an answer when I have my picture taken."

To George's amazement, Nancy encouraged the visit. Not having seen the woman they had followed to the séance, Nancy felt she might have gone to the studio.

By inquiring for directions from pedestrians, the girls arrived at length at a courtyard entered by means of a long passageway. At one side of it a flight of iron stairs led to a carved door which bore the photographer's sign.

"Up we go!" George laughed, starting ahead.

The studio, though old and a bit shabby, was well furnished. The proprietor, a short man with intent dark eyes and an artist's beret cocked over one ear, appeared so unusually eager that the girls wondered if he had many customers.

Nancy inquired the cost of having individual photographs made. The price was reasonable, so the three friends decided upon separate poses.

After the pictures had been taken, the photographer disappeared into the darkroom. Soon he returned with two dripping plates. The pictures on them of George and Bess were excellent. To

Bess's disappointment, however, not a trace of writing appeared on the glass.

"Where is my friend's picture?" inquired George, referring to Nancy.

The photographer returned to the darkroom for it. When Nancy glanced at the wet plate, she inhaled sharply. Just beneath her photograph were the words:

Beware your client's request.

"Spirit writing!" Bess gasped.

"Yes, a message from someone in the other world is warning you not to go on with your work," the photographer said slowly, with emphasis on the word "warning." "Young lady, do not take the warning lightly."

"No, I won't," said Nancy.

She had just glimpsed in the photographer's darkroom the woman they had seen on the plane! The next instant the door closed, and the lights in the studio went out. The room, with its one window heavily curtained, was in complete darkness.

A chill breeze suddenly wafted into the studio. Nancy felt a clammy hand brush across her face and fumble for her throat!

CHAPTER IV

A Strange Adventure

BESS screamed in terror. George, with more presence of mind, groped along the wall until she found a light switch she had noticed earlier. In another moment the room was bright again.

Both girls gasped in horror at what they saw. On the floor, almost at their feet, lay the photographer, unconscious! Bess started toward the man, but checked herself as George demanded:

"Where's Nancy?"

Their friend had vanished from the studio!

In their alarm, the cousins temporarily forgot the photographer. Frantically they ran into the darkroom, then into an adjoining kitchenette.

"Nancy!" George shouted. "Where are you?"

There was no answer.

"Nancy's gone and that photographer isn't regaining consciousness," Bess wailed. "What shall we do?"

"We must call the police," George decided.

Rushing out of the studio and down the iron steps, the girls ran through the deserted courtyard to the street. Fortunately, a policeman was less than half a block away. Hurrying up to him, George and Bess gasped out their story.

Immediately the patrolman accompanied the girls to the studio. As they entered, the photographer stirred slightly and sat up.

"What happened?" he mumbled.

"That's what we want to know," demanded the policeman. "What goes on here?"

"I was showing these girls a plate I'd just developed, when the lights went out. Something struck me on the head. That's all I remember."

"What became of the girl with us?" Bess asked.

The photographer, pulling himself on to a couch, gazed at her coldly and shrugged.

"How should I know?" he retorted.

"And where is the plate with the writing on it?" George suddenly demanded.

"The spirits must have been angry and taken it," the photographer said. "I've known them to do worse things than that."

The policeman appeared to be skeptical. He searched the building thoroughly, but no trace of Nancy or of the missing plate could be found.

Worried over Nancy's safety, and scarcely knowing what to do, Bess and George demanded the arrest of the photographer. The policeman, however, pointed out that they had no evidence against the photographer.

"Now don't you worry, young ladies. Your friend can't be far away. We'll have some detectives on the job right away. But I'll have to ask you to step around to the precinct station and give us a description of Nancy Drew."

Shortly afterward, Bess and George, considerably shaken, returned to their hotel. There, nervously pacing the floor, they debated whether to send a wire to River Heights.

"If Nancy doesn't show up in another half hour, we'd better notify Mr. Drew," Bess quavered. "To tell the truth, I'm so scared—"

"Listen!" George commanded.

Footsteps had sounded in the corridor, and now the door of the suite was opening. The two girls waited tensely. Nancy tottered in. Her hair was disheveled and her clothing wrinkled and soiled. Wearily she threw herself on the bed.

She greeted them with a wan smile. "Hello."

Bess and George ran to her solicitously. "Are you all right? What happened?"

Nancy told them how the hand had clutched at her throat when the lights went out in the studio.

"I tried to scream and couldn't. I was lifted bodily and carried out of the room."

"Where?" George asked.

"I couldn't see. A cold, wet cloth was clapped over my face. I was taken to the basement of a vacant house not far away and left there, bound hand and foot."

"How did you get away?" George questioned.

"I kept working until I was able to wriggle out of the cords. Then I climbed through a window and came straight here."

"Did you get the number of the house?" asked George. "I think we should get a policeman and investigate."

Nancy nodded. "We'll go to the police station as soon as I have a bath and change my clothes."

While Nancy was dressing, the girls discussed their recent experiences. George and Nancy were equally sure the photographer had resorted to trickery in putting the message on the plate.

"He could do it easily," George argued. "Maybe he used a plate which already had been exposed to the printed words."

"I believe there's more to it than that, George," Nancy told her. "I think the woman who spoke to us on the plane figures in it. I saw her at the studio," Nancy disclosed. "I'm convinced the photographer was part of a scheme and only pretended to be knocked unconscious. We must get that plate with the message on it."

"It's gone," said George.

This news added to Nancy's suspicions about the whole adventure. As soon as she was dressed, the girls returned to the police station, and an officer was assigned to accompany them. A careful search was made of the vacant building where Nancy had been imprisoned, but not a clue could be found. Even the cords which had bound her had disappeared.

To their surprise the policeman remarked soberly, "This isn't the first time queer things have happened in this section of the city."

No additional information was gained by calling on the photographer, who maintained his innocence in the affair. Bess and George obtained their pictures, but the man insisted that the plate with the spirit writing had disappeared.

When the girls were in their hotel suite once more, George remarked, "Queer about the warning message—'Beware your client's request.' Do you think it meant Mrs. Putney's case?"

"I'm sure it does. But," Nancy said with a determined smile, "now I'll work even harder to solve the mystery!"

"Nancy," said Bess, "is there anything else we can do down here? I feel we should go home and report to Mrs. Putney."

"Maybe she's had another message!" said George.

"Do you suppose she goes to séances?" Bess asked, "and then later dreams she's hearing her husband talk to her?"

"It's possible," Nancy replied. "But it would be hard to get her to admit it."

Bess and George were glad to leave New Orleans. Nancy's experience had frightened them, and they felt that some sinister motive was back of her temporary abduction. Nancy herself was reluctant to leave.

"I think several people were involved in an effort to get me out of the way so that I couldn't find out too much," she said.

Despite the danger, she thought a further search should be made for the mysterious woman. Yet she agreed there was some justice in the girls' argument that Mrs. Putney should be consulted.

Learning that a plane which stopped at River Heights left within an hour, the girls quickly packed and reached the airport just in time. The trip home was uneventful, but during the flight, Bess revealed that she had a little mystery.

"That's what I wanted to ask Amurah," said Bess. "You remember Mrs. White, who comes to our house once a week to clean? She has a daughter, Lola, who is eighteen. Her mother's terribly worried about her."

Nancy recalled the woman, a very gentle, patient person who had suffered a great deal of misfortune. At present her husband was in a sanatorium, and she was struggling to pay the debts his illness had piled up.

"Where does the mystery come in?" Nancy asked.

It seemed that lately, Lola, ordinarily good-natured and jolly, had become unnaturally subdued. She acted as if she were living in a dream world. Mrs. White said there had been no broken romance, nor had her daughter lost her job.

"In fact," said Bess, "Lola earns good wages at a factory and used to give her mother most of the money. Now she gives her practically nothing but won't say why. Something has happened to her," Bess insisted. "Oh, Nancy, won't you go to see Lola? Maybe she'll tell you what's wrong."

"All right, I will," Nancy promised.

Nancy kept her promise the day after she returned from New Orleans. After calling Mrs. Putney and making an appointment for the following day, she started for Lola White's home, wondering what she would say.

Evidently Bess had told Mrs. White she might expect the visit from Nancy. No sooner had Nancy rapped, than the door was opened by Lola's mother. It was evident that she had been crying.

"Oh, Nancy, I'm so relieved you've come!" she said, her voice trembling. "Lola didn't go to work today. Ever since breakfast she's acted like someone in a trance. Please see if you can do something for her!"

CHAPTER V

The Figure in White

"LOLA dear, Nancy Drew is here to see you," called Mrs. White.

The woman had led the way to the back yard, where her daughter sat motionless, staring into space.

"It is quite useless," sighed Mrs. White. "She will talk to no one."

"Oh, Lola needn't talk," Nancy said in a friendly voice. "I came to take her for a little ride in the country. It's a beautiful day."

"Yes, it is!" Mrs. White agreed. "Lola, wouldn't you like to go for a ride, dear?"

Lola, though looking none too pleased, made no protest. Once in the car, she sat in silence, gazing ahead as if hypnotized.

Nancy pretended to pay no attention as the car sped along the picturesque river road. The prolonged stillness seemed to wear upon Lola, who kept pushing back her long blond hair. Several times she glanced at Nancy. Finally, unable to bear the strain, she asked:

"Why did you bring me out here?"

"To help you if I can." Nancy smiled. "You're worried about something to do with money, aren't you? Is it about your job?"

"Well, sort of," Lola confessed. "It's just that my wages at the factory aren't mine any—" She broke off and gazed forlornly at Nancy.

"Why not tell me everything?" Nancy urged. "Perhaps I can help you."

"No one can. I've pledged to give away almost every cent I earn."

"Whatever induced you to do that, Lola? To whom are you giving the money?"

"I can't tell you," the girl replied, her head low and her voice scarcely above a whisper.

"Do you feel that's fair to your mother? She must need part of your earnings."

"That's what worries me," Lola said miserably. "I've pledged myself and I can't get out of it. I don't dare tell Mother the truth either. Oh, I'm in a mess! I wish I were dead!"

"Now that's silly talk! We'll find a way out of this. If I were you I'd ignore the pledge."

"I don't dare," Lola said fearfully.

Nancy told her that any legitimate organization would not take money to the point of depriving

Mrs. White of needed support. If Lola were paying money to unscrupulous persons, she should have no qualms about breaking the pledge.

"You really think so? If only I dared!"

"I'm sure that your mother would tell you the same thing."

"I guess you're right," Lola admitted. "Maybe I've been foolish."

For another half hour, Nancy talked to the girl in a friendly way, seeking to learn to whom she had pledged her salary. Lola, however, would not reveal the information.

When Nancy finally drove her home, Lola thanked her and promised to follow her advice. The next day Nancy was pleased to hear from Bess that Lola White seemed to be herself again.

"Splendid!" Nancy commented. "I only hope whoever was taking her money will leave her alone now."

As soon as Bess had gone, Nancy hurried to the widow's home. Mrs. Putney herself opened the front door of the big house.

"Oh, I'm so glad you came," she cried excitedly. "While you were gone I remembered something I had forgotten to tell you. In the directions given me by my dear husband as to where I should conceal my jewelry, he mentioned specifically that I was to look for a sign of three twigs placed on the ground and that I should bury the jewel case two steps from the sign in the direction of the big walnut tree. When I reached the clearing I found the three twigs lying crossed on the ground, just as the spirit had directed me."

"Oh, Mrs. Putney, I wish you had told me about this when we were at the spot before!" exclaimed Nancy.

She glanced at her wrist watch. "It's only four o'clock. I'll pick up my friends and drive out now to see if the crossed twigs are still there."

When the girls reached the clearing in the woods, there lay the three crossed twigs. The position seemed too perfect for Nature to have placed them there. Yet Nancy doubted that they were the same ones which Mrs. Putney had seen. Rain and wind would have displaced the others.

"The thief may use this method to communicate with his confederates," Nancy mused. "But why would—"

Her voice trailed off. Through the trees Nancy had seen a flash of white.

"Someone's over there," Bess whispered uneasily.

"Let's try to get closer without being seen!" George urged.

Taking care not to step on dry twigs, the girls entered the woods. Through the bushes, they could see the back of a young woman with long blond hair.

"That almost looks like Lola White!" Nancy exclaimed.

The girl appeared to be reaching high into the crotch of a black walnut tree.

"She's hiding something there!" Nancy whispered excitedly.

The girl suddenly moved off in the opposite direction. Soon she disappeared.

Nancy went quickly to the big walnut. Standing on tiptoe, she reached into a hollow in the trunk of the tree. Triumphantly she pulled out a sealed envelope. The others crowded around her.

The envelope bore no name or address, but on its face was a crude drawing of three crossed twigs!

"Wow!" said George. "The mystery deepens!"

"What's inside?" Bess asked in awe.

"If I had one guess, I'd say money," Nancy replied. "I feel justified in opening it, too, for I'm sure it was meant for the person who stole Mrs. Putney's jewelry."

The other girls agreed. Carefully Nancy slipped her thumb under the flap, gradually peeling it free. Inside was a sheet of paper and ten five-dollar bills.

There was no message but the name "Sadie." So the girl had not been Lola!

"I wonder who the girl was," said George.

"What I want to know is why she left the money here," said Nancy. "We must overtake her and find out!" On second thought she added, "Maybe the thief will come to the tree to get the envelope. I'll stay here. You two go."

"She's hiding something!" Nancy whispered

The cousins darted off, leaving Nancy alone beside the black walnut tree. Carefully Nancy put the envelope back in the hollow, and sat down a little distance away to watch.

As Nancy sat with her back to a tree trunk, she thought she heard the soft pad of steps. She straightened up, listening intently, but heard nothing.

"Probably some animal," Nancy decided.

Nevertheless, she glanced about carefully. Her skin prickled, as if in warning that some stranger might be nearby.

"Nerves!" she told herself.

At that moment Bess and George, unsuccessful in their pursuit of the blond girl, were returning. Coming within view of the big walnut tree, George was astonished to see a strange sight. Though no wind was blowing, a leafless branch of a tree behind the walnut seemed to bend slowly downward.

"Bess, look—" she began, then ended lamely, "Never mind! It's gone now."

"What's gone?" Bess demanded.

"A branch. I guess my eyes tricked me," George admitted.

Hearing the voices of her friends, Nancy quickly arose and came to meet them. Seeing that they were alone, she said in disappointment:

"You weren't able to overtake her?"

"We had miserable luck," Bess admitted. "We didn't even get close enough to see her face."

"We trailed her to the main highway, where she must have hopped a bus," George added.

"I think we should take the money with us," Nancy said. "I'll ask Dad what to do about it."

On tiptoe, Nancy reached into the hollow of the tree. A puzzled expression came over her face.

"The envelope's gone!" she exclaimed.

"It can't be!" insisted Bess.

Nancy groped again and shook her head. "The envelope is gone! But no one was here!"

"I've got an idea," said George. "Maybe someone climbed another tree, crossed over into the big walnut, and then snatched the letter from above!"

"The trees are so close together I suppose it could be done," Nancy admitted doubtfully.

"Wait a minute," George cried out excitedly. Then she told about the slowly bending, leafless branch.

Nancy peered intently up into the old walnut and the maple next to it. "No one there," she observed. "George, you're sure it was a branch and not a fish pole with a hook on the end that was used?" she asked.

"It could have been a pole."

"I understand several things now!" Nancy exclaimed, thinking aloud. "That metal object I saw near here the other day must have been part of a collapsible pole! I'll bet it belonged to the same person who was here today!"

"And the same one who robbed Mrs. Putney!" added Bess.

"George, did the stick bend down out of the tree, or did it come from the direction of the bushes?" Nancy asked.

"I couldn't see well enough to be sure," George replied. "But from where I stood, it appeared to bend down out of a tree behind the walnut."

The three went back to the convertible, agreeing that it might be a good idea to keep a lookout for visitors to the walnut tree. Obviously it was being used as a collection station by someone extracting money from gullible people.

Later, as she drove homeward, Nancy began to wonder whether this might not tie in with Lola White's peculiar actions.

As she turned into her own driveway she noticed a dark-green sports car parked in front. The driver came to meet her.

"Hi, Nancy!" Ned grinned. "Guess I got here a little early."

"I'm late. Been working on a case. Please forgive me."

A week earlier she had accepted Ned Nickerson's invitation to a sundown picnic planned by Emerson College students spending their summer in River Heights.

"I'll be ready in fifteen minutes," she promised.

While Ned waited on the porch, she rushed into the house, showered, and dressed. On her way downstairs, she paused in the kitchen to say good-by to Mrs. Gruen.

"It seems to me you're never home any more," the housekeeper replied. But she added with a smile, "Have a good time and put mystery out of that pretty head for tonight!"

"How could I?" Nancy laughed gaily.

Nancy had not asked Ned where the picnic was to be held. Therefore, she was surprised when she discovered that the spot selected was on the upper Muskoka River, less than a mile from the mysterious walnut tree.

"Want to do me a favor?" she asked Ned.

"Sure thing."

Nancy told him about the money in the walnut tree, its puzzling disappearance, and her suspicion that something sinister was going on.

"And you want to stop and have a look for more envelopes," said Ned. "Okay."

They found nothing in the tree, but the crossed twigs had been removed. Someone had been there! Ned promised to stop at the spot now and then to see if he could learn anything.

They drove on to the picnic spot, where their friends had already gathered. The aroma of broiling hamburgers made them ravenous.

Both Nancy and Ned were favorites among

their friends, and soon everyone was laughing and joking. After all the food had been consumed, some of the young people began to sing. Others went off in canoes.

"Let's go out on the river, Nancy," Ned suggested.

Nancy sat in the bow of the canoe, her paddle lying idle across the gunwales, while Ned paddled smoothly upstream. Moonlight streamed over the treetops and shimmered across the surface of the water. Presently Ned guided the canoe into a cove and let it glide silently toward shore.

"What a night!" he said. "I wish—"

Suddenly Nancy, who was facing the shore, sat bolt upright and uttered a low cry.

"Look over there, Ned!" she exclaimed in a hushed voice. "Am I seeing things?"

The youth, who had been watching the moonlight on the water, turned his head and was startled to see a ghostly white figure wading out into the river from the beach.

"Whew!" Ned caught his breath, nearly dropping his paddle.

As the canoe swung with the current, Nancy got a clear view of the figure in white.

The person wading deeper and deeper into the water was Lola White!

CHAPTER VI

A New Lead

"QUICK, Ned!" Nancy cried, seizing her paddle. "She'll be in over her head in a minute. We must save her!"

Her companion needed no urging. He sent the canoe forward with powerful strokes.

"Lola, stay where you are! Don't move!" Nancy called to her.

The girl did not appear to hear. On she waded, holding her hands in front of her.

As Nancy had feared, the shallow water ended abruptly. The next instant Lola had stepped in over her head. The ducking seemed to bring her out of her trance, and now she began to struggle frantically. If she knew how to swim, she gave no evidence of it.

Fortunately, the canoe was soon alongside her. Quickly Ned eased himself into the water, while Nancy steadied the craft. He seized the struggling and terrified girl, then began to swim toward shore. In a moment they were in shallow water.

Nancy was waiting with the canoe, and the sputtering Lola was lifted into the bottom of the craft. The girl was only half conscious. Nancy bent low over her and caught the words, "the beckoning hand."

"Gosh!" Ned observed uneasily. "She's in a bad way!"

"We must get her home right away," Nancy decided. "And you, too, with those wet clothes."

Paddling as fast as they could, she and Ned started toward the picnic grounds where he had left his car. Midway there, Lola seemed to recover her senses. She sat up and gazed at Nancy as if recognizing her for the first time.

"Lola, why were you wading out into the water?" Nancy asked.

"I can't tell you," Lola answered weakly.

"You said something about a beckoning hand."

"I did?" Lola's eyes opened wide and an expression of horror came over her face.

"You thought someone was calling to you?"

Lola spoke with an effort. "I'm grateful to you for pulling me out of the river. But I can't answer your questions!"

Nancy said no more. Taking off her sweater, she put it around the shivering girl.

Later, when they reached the picnic grounds, she hurried Lola in secret to Ned's car, as the college group made joking remarks to Ned about his bedraggled appearance.

At the White home Nancy and Ned lingered only long enough to be certain that Lola had suffered no ill effects from her immersion.

"Please don't tell anyone what happened," Mrs. White pleaded. "Lola went out this evening without telling me where she was going. I can't imagine why she would go to the river."

"Perhaps to meet someone," Nancy suggested.

"So far as I know, she had no date. Oh, I do so need your help to clear up this mystery, Nancy!"

"I'll do everything I can," Nancy promised.

Upon returning home, the young detective sat for a long while in the Drew library, reflecting upon the events of the evening.

Nancy mused also about the many unrelated incidents that had taken place the past week. Into several of these the mysterious Howard Brex seemed to fit very naturally. Yet of his whereabouts since his release from prison, nothing was known.

Penning a brief note to Mr. Johnson, Brex's former boss in New Orleans, she described the crossed-twig sign, and asked if by chance it had any connection with the suspect and his jewelry designs.

For several days after the letter had been sent, Nancy and her friends kept a fairly close watch on the black walnut tree at the edge of the clearing.

But so far as they could determine, no one visited the tree, either to leave money or to take it away.

"We're wasting time watching this place," Ned commented after the third day. "Whoever it is you're looking for knows you've discovered the walnut-tree cache, and has probably moved to a safer locality."

Nancy was inclined to agree with him. She felt very discouraged, for it seemed that she was making no progress whatever in solving the stolen jewelry mystery. Because she could report no success to Mrs. Putney, she avoided calling upon her.

But a letter from Mr. Johnson, the jewelry manufacturer, brought startling results. He wrote:

The crossed-twig design you described was never used in any work Brex did for us. We have also looked through other jewelers' catalogs, but do not find anything like this design pictured.

However, some time ago, a simple-minded janitor in this office building received from Chicago a letter bearing an insigne of crossed twigs. The man was urged to invest money in stock of the Three Branch Ranch on the promise of doubling his funds. The scheme sounded dishonest, and I persuaded him to ignore it. I would have reported the stock sellers to the authorities, but unfortunately the janitor destroyed the letter before I had a chance to examine it.

Nancy took Mr. Johnson's letter to her father, who read it carefully, then offered a suggestion.

"Why not notify the postal authorities? It's against the law, as you know, to use the mail to promote dishonest schemes."

"Will you do it for me, Dad? Your letterhead is so impressive!"

"All right, I'll dictate a letter to my secretary this afternoon," the lawyer promised.

Nancy decided to write a letter of her own to the Government Information Service to inquire if they had any record of a Three Branch Ranch. Three days later she received a reply. She was told that no such ranch was listed.

"This practically makes it certain the stock scheme is a swindle!" she declared. "The headquarters of the outfit may be in Chicago, but I'll bet salesmen are working in other places." Yet it was difficult for her to connect Brex, a clever designer of jewelry, with a crooked stock promotion.

Even though she had no conclusive information to convey, Nancy decided to call upon Mrs. Putney to ask a few questions. Just as she was about to leave the house, however, a taxi stopped in front, and the widow herself alighted.

Mrs. Putney looked even more worried than on the previous occasion.

"Poor thing," Nancy said to herself. "I'd like to be able to help her!"

Nancy met Mrs. Putney at the front door, and cordially escorted her into the living room.

"I've come to see you, because you never come to my house," the visitor scolded Nancy mildly.

"I haven't been to see you lately, because I had nothing to report, Mrs. Putney. I intended to call today."

"Then I'll forgive you, my dear. If you were coming, you must have a clue."

"Several of them, I hope. Before I tell you what I suspect, I must ask you a rather personal question, Mrs. Putney. Do you own any stock in the Three Branch Ranch?"

Nancy's question seemed to take the widow completely by surprise.

"What—what do you know about the Three Branch Ranch?" she asked in a voice which quavered with emotion. Her faded eyes reflected stark fear.

CHAPTER VII

Matching Wits

ALARMED, Nancy called to Hannah Gruen, who came in hurriedly from the garden. Then she took Mrs. Putney's arm and led her to a chair.

"I didn't mean to upset you," said Nancy. "Please sit down, and Hannah will bring you a cup of tea."

While Mrs. Gruen was in the kitchen preparing the tea, Mrs. Putney rested quietly.

"How did you discover—about the ranch?" she finally asked in a voice scarcely above a whisper.

Nancy remained silent as the widow slumped back in her chair. When the housekeeper brought her a cup of tea, she sipped it obediently. Presently she declared she felt much better.

"Please forgive me for having distressed you so," begged Nancy.

"On the contrary, I should have told you sooner. Three days ago I had another message from my dear husband. He advised me to invest my money in a good, sound stock. Three Branch Ranch was recommended. That's why I was so startled when you asked me about it, Nancy."

"The message came to you at home?" Nancy inquired.

"No, through a medium. I heard of the woman and attended a séance at her home. It was very satisfying."

"Who is she, and where does she live?"

The question took Mrs. Putney by surprise. "Why, I don't know," she said.

"You don't know!" exclaimed Nancy. "Then how could you attend a séance in her home?"

"I learned of the woman through a friendly note which came in the mail. The message said if I cared to attend the séance, I should meet a car which would call for me that night."

"The car came?"

"Yes. It was driven by a woman who wore a dark veil. During a rather long ride into the country, she never once spoke to me."

"Yet you weren't uneasy or suspicious?"

"It all seemed in keeping with what I had understood to be the general practice in such things. The ride was a long one, and I fell asleep. When I awakened, the car stood in front of a dark house."

"You were taken inside?"

"Yes. The veiled woman escorted me to a room illuminated by only a dim, greenish light. When my eyes became accustomed to it, I saw a white, filmily clad figure lying on a couch. Through this medium, the spirit of my husband spoke to me."

At the recollection, Mrs. Putney began to tremble again.

"Your husband advised you to invest money in the Three Branch Ranch!" Nancy said. "What else did he tell you?"

"That I should listen to no advice from any earthly person, and keep what he told me to myself. Oh, dear!"

"What's the matter?" Nancy asked kindly.

"I've told too much already! I shouldn't have revealed a word of this to anyone!"

The widow arose and in an agitated voice asked Nancy to call a taxi.

"I'll drive you home myself," Nancy offered.

During the ride, the young detective avoided further reference to the subject which so distressed her companion. But as she left the widow at her doorstep, she said casually:

"I suppose you did invest money in Three Branch Ranch?"

"Only a little. I gave what cash I had with me to the medium, who promised to use it to purchase the stock for me."

"I don't like to worry you, Mrs. Putney, but I'm afraid you may lose the money you invested."

"Oh, I couldn't. My husband's judgment on business matters was excellent!"

"I don't question that, Mrs. Putney. But I have evidence which convinces me you were tricked by a group of clever swindlers."

Nancy then told of the letter she had received from the Government Information Service, saying no Three Branch Ranch was listed, and that the postal authorities had been notified.

"Promise me you'll not invest another penny until the outfit can be thoroughly investigated."

"I trust your judgment," the widow said. "I promise."

"And another thing. May I have the note you received telling of the séance?"

"I haven't it. I was requested to return it to the medium as evidence of my good faith."

"Oh, that's a bad break for us," Nancy said in disappointment. "Those fakers think of everything! The letter might have provided a clue!"

"What can we do?"

"Don't admit that you suspect trickery," Nancy advised. "Sooner or later, another séance will be suggested and you will be requested to invest more of your money. Phone me the minute you receive another communication."

"Oh, I will!" Mrs. Putney promised.

After leaving the widow, Nancy began to speculate on how many others in River Heights might have been duped into buying the phony stock. The first one to come into her mind was Lola White. The second was the mysterious Sadie.

"Lola probably signed up for a lot of stock, and is paying the bill little by little, out of her wages," Nancy surmised. "I must see her at once."

Lola was not at her place of employment. Upon being told that the girl had not appeared for work that day because of illness, Nancy drove to the White cottage. Lola was lying in a hammock on the front porch, gazing morosely at the ceiling. She sat up and tried to look cheerful.

"How are you today?" Nancy inquired. "No bad effects from the river?"

"I'm all right, I guess," Lola answered. "Thanks for what you did."

"We were just fortunate to be there when you needed us," replied Nancy. "By the way, do you feel like telling me why you were there?"

"No, I don't," Lola said sullenly.

Nancy did not press the matter. Instead, she asked her if she had ever heard of the Three Branch Ranch. Lola's eyebrows shot up, but she shook her head.

Then Nancy told Lola that her real purpose in coming to call was to ask if she were acquainted with a girl named Sadie.

"Oh, you must mean the one who works at the Save-A-Lot Market," Lola said. "I don't know her last name."

"Thanks a lot, Lola. I'll go to see her." As Nancy went down the porch steps she added, "Keep your chin up, Lola!"

Happy that she had obtained a lead, Nancy climbed into her convertible, waved to Lola, and sped away down the street.

When Nancy inquired at the market whether a girl named Sadie worked there, a tall blonde operating a cash register was pointed out. So busy that she was in no mood to talk, the girl frowned as Nancy paused and spoke to her.

"You're Sadie?" Nancy asked, uncomfortably aware that she was delaying a line of customers.

"Sadie Bond," the girl replied briskly.

"I'm trying to trace a Sadie interested in buying stock in a western ranch," Nancy said, keeping her voice low.

"You've got the wrong girl, miss," Sadie replied. "I don't have money to buy ranches."

Nancy smiled. "Then I guess I'm looking for some other person."

Having drawn a blank, Nancy decided that her next move should be to write an advertisement for the River Heights *Gazette*.

It read:

> *SADIE: If you are blonde and know of a certain walnut tree, a beautiful gift awaits you in return for information. Reply Box 358.*

The second day after the advertisement appeared, Nancy, with Bess and George, went to the *Gazette* office to ask if there had been any replies.

To their astonishment, nearly a dozen letters were handed them.

"Jumping jellyfish!" muttered George. "How many walnut-tree Sadies are there in this town?"

Carrying the replies to a nearby park, the girls divided the letters and sat down to read them. Several were from pranksters, or persons who obviously had no information about the walnut tree but were eager to obtain a free gift.

"Running that ad was a waste of money," Bess sighed, tossing aside her last letter.

Nancy, however, was deeply engrossed in a letter written on the stationery of the Lovelee Cosmetic Company. "Girls, listen to this!" she exclaimed.

" 'I have blond hair. Do you refer to a black walnut tree along the Muskoka River? What is the gift you are offering? Sadie Green.' "

"We must find out more about this girl right away!" Nancy declared.

She telephoned the cosmetic firm and learned that Sadie was the telephone operator. When Nancy spoke about the letter, the girl pleaded with her not to come to the office.

"I'll meet you in the park," Sadie promised. "I'll be there in a few minutes."

The three friends were afraid the girl might not keep her promise. But eventually they saw a young woman with long blond hair approaching.

"I can't stay more than a minute," she said nervously. "The boss would have a fit if he knew I skipped out!"

"Will you answer a few questions?"

"What do you want to know?"

"First, tell me, did you ever hear of the Three Branch Ranch?"

"Never," the girl replied with a blank look.

"Did you leave an envelope with money in the hollow of a tree near the river?" Nancy asked.

The girl moved a step away. "Who are you?" she mumbled. "Detectives? Why do you ask me such a thing?" Before Nancy could reply, she burst out, "I've changed my mind. Keep your present!"

With a frightened look in her eyes, Sadie whirled and ran off through the park.

"That girl is afraid to tell what she knows!" Nancy exclaimed. "But we may learn something by talking to her parents."

Inquiry at the Lovelee personnel department brought forth the information that Sadie lived with an elderly grandfather, Charles Green, on North James Street. The girls went directly there.

Old Mr. Green sat on the front porch in a rocker, reading a newspaper. He laid the paper aside as the girls came up the walk.

"You friends o' my granddaughter Sadie?" he asked in a friendly way. "She ain't here now."

"We're acquaintances of Sadie," Nancy replied, seating herself on the porch railing.

"If you're aimin' to get her to go some place with you, I calculate it won't do no good to ask." The old man sighed. "Sadie's actin' kinda peculiar lately."

"In what way?" Nancy asked with interest.

"Oh, she's snappish-like when I ask her questions," the old man revealed. "She ain't bringin' her money home like she used to, either."

Mr. Green, who seemed eager for companionship, chatted on about Sadie. She was a good girl, he said, but lately he could not figure her out.

From the conversation, Nancy was convinced that the case of Sadie Green was very similar to that of Lola White. After the girls had left the house, Nancy proposed that they drive out to the black walnut.

"I have a plan," she said.

Nancy did not say what it was, but after examining the hollow in the walnut tree, which was empty, she looked all about her. Then she tore a sheet from a notebook in her purse. Using very bad spelling, she printed:

> *My girl friend told me by leaving a letter hear I can get in touch with a pursen who can give infermation. Please oblige. Yours, Ruby Brown, Genral Delivry, River Heights.*

"You hope to trap the man who took the fifty dollars!" George exclaimed admiringly. "But how do you know you'll get an answer? It seems pretty definite that the racketeers aren't using this tree as a post office any longer."

"We'll have to take a chance," said Nancy. "And if there is an answer, someone will have to call for it who answers to the name of 'Ruby Brown.' "

"George and I will," Bess offered eagerly.

Nancy smilingly shook her head. "You're well known as my friends. No, I'll have a stranger call for the letter, so that anyone assigned to watch the post office won't become suspicious."

Nancy arranged with a laundress, who sometimes worked at the Drew home, to inquire for the letter each day.

"Did you get it?" Nancy asked eagerly when Belinda returned the third day.

The good-natured laundress, lips parted in a wide grin, said, "I got it, Miss Nancy!"

Taking the letter, Nancy ran upstairs to her room to open it in private. She gasped when she read the message enclosed, which was:

If you're on the level, Ruby, go to Humphrey's Black Walnut for instructions. If you are a disbeliever, may the wrath of all the Humphreys descend upon you!

CHAPTER VIII

The Ghost at the Organ

REREADING the message several times, Nancy speculated about the Humphreys and their connection with the black walnut tree.

Deciding it best to keep the contents of the message to herself, Nancy went to the River Heights Public Library, hoping to find a book which would throw some light on the Humphreys mentioned in the note. The name sounded vaguely familiar, and it had occurred to her that it might belong to one of the very old families of the county.

Finally Nancy found exactly the book she wanted. Fascinated, she read that a famous old walnut grove along the river once had been known as Humphrey's Woods.

Even more exciting was the information that a duel, fatal to one member of the family, had been fought beneath a certain walnut tree. The tree, known since then as Humphrey's Walnut, was marked with a plaque.

The article went on to say that Blackwood Hall, the family home, was still standing. Built of walnut from the woods surrounding it, the mansion had, in its day, been one of the showplaces along the river. Now the grounds were weed-grown, the old home vacant, and the family gone.

"It seems a pity to neglect a fine old place that way," Nancy thought. "Why would—"

The next sentence aroused her curiosity.

"It is rumored that Jonathan's ghost still inhabits the place!"

Nancy decided she must investigate Blackwood Hall, although she smiled at the thought of any ghost walking there.

But first she would find Humphrey's Walnut. When she returned home, Nancy telephoned Ned, asking if he were free to accompany her, and told him briefly about the letter.

"I'll pick you up in my car in five minutes!" he promised eagerly.

At Nancy's direction, Ned drove as close as he could to the ancient walnut grove by the river. Then they parked the car and started off on foot. They examined each tree for a plaque. It was not until they were deep in the grove that Nancy spied the dull bronze marker with its tragic account of how Jonathan Humphrey had died in a duel while defending his honor beneath the shade of that tree. For fully a minute neither Nancy nor Ned spoke; then Nancy's voice shook off the spell of the place.

"I wonder if anyone will come," said Nancy.

"The note suggested that you were to receive instructions of some kind," Ned remarked.

"Perhaps this tree, also, is used to hold messages. Do you see any hollow in the trunk, Ned?"

The youth, noticing a deep pocket in the crotch of the walnut, ran his hand into it.

"Say, something's crammed in here!" he said excitedly. "Yes, it's a paper!"

"And addressed to Ruby Brown!" Nancy cried, looking at it.

The message was short.

Name the girl friend who suggested you leave that letter.

"Wow!" exclaimed Ned. "Looks as if you've put your foot in it now, Nancy."

Nancy read the message again, then asked Ned to put it back. "Come on!" she urged.

Nancy led the way back to the car and they drove to the walnut tree where she had left her first note signed "Ruby Brown." Again Nancy printed a badly spelled message, asking for instructions on how to find the Humphrey tree.

"That ought to fool him." She chuckled as Ned placed the note in the hollow of the tree. "He'll think poor Ruby is dumb, which is exactly what I want him to think."

"Say, why don't you ask the police to guard the place?"

"Because I'm afraid I'll scare off the man altogether. I want to trap the mastermind behind this thing, not some errand boy."

For the next two days, no mail was received by General Delivery for Ruby Brown. On the third morning, in response to Nancy's telephone call, she learned a letter was at the post office. The laundress went to get it.

"What does our unknown friend write this time?" asked Bess, who had arrived at the Drew home just ahead of the maid. "Does he tell Ruby how to reach the Humphrey Walnut?"

"He says 'Ask Lola White.' "

"Lola!" exclaimed Bess. "That poor girl! Then she *is* involved in that swindler's scheme."

"I've suspected it all along," Nancy admitted. "The fellow is clever. He's suspicious that Ruby Brown is a hoax, but so far I don't think he connects her with me in any way. And it's my job to keep him from finding out."

"What will you do next?" asked Bess. "Talk to Lola?"

"Not right away," Nancy decided. "Unwittingly she might carry the information back to the writer of this note."

"Then what's the next move?"

"Dad says when you're confused—and I admit I am—you should sit back and try to arrange the facts into some kind of order," Nancy replied. "Dad also thinks a change of scenery is a good idea when you're in a mental jam."

"Where shall we go?" asked Bess.

"How would you like to go with me to Blackwood Hall?" asked Nancy. "The book at the library told various stories about this old mansion, which stands within a few miles of River Heights. It's haunted, has a secret tunnel, and is said to house the ghost of one Jonathan Humphrey who lost his life in a duel. Would you like to explore it with me?"

At first Bess insisted that wild horses could not drag her to the deserted mansion. But later, when she learned that Nancy had persuaded George to accompany her, she weakened in her decision.

"I'll go along," she said. "But I'm sure we're headed for trouble."

The trio set off at once, although a summer storm seemed to be brewing. As the girls tramped through the woods along the river, Nancy suddenly stopped short. Below her was the cove where she and Ned had rescued Lola White. The girls were not far from Blackwood Hall now. Could there be any connection between the sinister old place and the strange, hypnotic state in which they had found Lola that night?

Without voicing her thoughts to the others,

Nancy plunged on. At last they came within view of the ancient building. The three-story mansion, where several generations of Humphreys had lived, looked as black as its name, forbidding even by daylight. High weeds and grass choked off any paths that might once have led to the house.

The girls circled the mansion. The wind rattled the shutters and at intervals whistled dismally around the corners of the great structure. An open gate to what had once been a flower garden slammed back and forth, as if moved by an unseen hand.

Nancy walked to the massive front door, expecting to find it securely fastened. To her amazement, as she turned the knob, the door slowly opened on groaning hinges.

"Well, what do you know!" George muttered.

Bess tried to dissuade her friends from going inside, but they paid no attention.

Turning on flashlights, the three girls entered the big hall into which the door opened. The floor was richly carpeted, but Time had played its part in making the carpet worn and gray with mildew.

Velvet draperies, faded and rotted, hung from the windows of an adjoining room. Through the archway, the girls caught a glimpse of a few massive pieces of walnut furniture.

"This looks interesting," Nancy observed. "There's nothing to be afraid of here."

At that moment the front door banged shut behind them. Bess stifled a scream of terror.

"Goose! It was only the wind!" George scolded her. "If you keep this up, you'll give us all a case of the jitters."

"I'm sorry," said Bess, "but it's so spooky."

Just then a sound of sudden, heavy rain told the girls a storm had indeed begun.

Passing through what they took to be a small parlor, the girls found themselves in another long hall, running at right angles to the entrance hall. From it opened a huge room, so dark that their flashlights illuminated only a small section of it.

"Listen!" Nancy whispered suddenly.

As they paused in the doorway, the three distinctly heard the sound of organ music. Bess seized George's arm in a viselike grip.

"W-what's that?" she quavered. "It must be ghost music!"

"It couldn't be—" George began, but the words died in her throat.

At the end of the room a weird, greenish light began to glow. It revealed a small organ.

At the keyboard of the instrument sat a luminous figure.

Bess uttered a terrified shriek which echoed through the ancient house. Instantly the dim light vanished, and the music died away. The long room was in darkness.

Nancy raised her flashlight and ran toward the place where the phantom organist had appeared. Only the old, dust-covered organ remained against the wall.

"It looks as if it hadn't been touched for years," Nancy remarked.

"Oh, Nancy! Let's leave this dreadful place!" Bess wailed from across the room. "The house is haunted! Somebody's ghost does live here!"

Refusing to listen to her friends' pleas to wait, Bess rapidly retreated. A solid slamming of the front door told them she was safely out of the house.

George, keeping her voice low, commented, "To tell the truth, I'm a little nervous, too."

"So am I," admitted Nancy. "This place is haunted all right—not by a specter but by a very live and perhaps dangerous person."

"How did that 'ghost,' or whatever it was, get out of the room so fast? And without passing us?"

"That's what we must find out," Nancy replied, focusing her light on the walls again. "There may be a secret exit that the—"

She ended in midsentence as a girl's piercing scream reached their ears. The cry came from outside the mansion.

"That was Bess!" Nancy exclaimed.

Fearful, the two girls abandoned the search and

raced outdoors. The rain was coming down in torrents, making it difficult to see far ahead.

At first they could not locate Bess anywhere. Then Nancy caught a glimpse of her, huddled among the trees a few yards away. She was trembling violently.

"A man!" Bess chattered as her companions ran up to her. "I saw him!"

"Did you get a good look at him?" Nancy asked.

Bess had been too frightened to do this. But she was sure she must have surprised the person who had come from the direction of the house, for he had turned abruptly and entered the woods.

"Any chance of overtaking him?" Nancy questioned.

"Oh, no!" Bess had no desire either to lead or join an expedition through the woods. "He's gone. He knows his way and we don't. Let's go home, girls. We're wet through, and we'll catch colds."

"I'm going back to the mansion," Nancy announced.

"I'll come along," said George. "We'll hunt again for the hidden exit that the ghost at the organ must have taken!"

Bess reluctantly accompanied her friends. As they reached the massive front door, Nancy noticed that it was closed.

"I'm sure I left it open. The wind must have blown it shut," she remarked.

George tried to open the door. Though she twisted the knob in both directions and pushed hard, the door refused to budge.

"Bolted from inside," George concluded. "The ghost isn't anxious for company."

"I can't get it out of my mind that Blackwood Hall is part of this whole mixed-up mystery," Nancy remarked thoughtfully. "I wish I could get inside again!"

Nancy smiled to herself. Ned was coming to dinner. She would ask him to bring her back to Blackwood Hall that evening. Ghosts were always supposed to perform better at night!

"All right, let's go," she said cheerfully.

Before returning home, Nancy did a few errands, so it was after six o'clock when she reached her own house. Hannah Gruen opened the door excitedly.

"Mrs. Putney has been trying all afternoon to reach you by telephone. She wants to talk to you about something very important."

"I believe Mrs. Putney is going to attend another séance!" Nancy exclaimed.

Nancy hurried to the telephone and called the Putney number, but there was no answer.

"Oh, dear, I hope she won't be taken in again by the faker," Nancy said to herself.

Without the slightest clue as to where to find

Mrs. Putney, Nancy turned her thoughts toward the evening's plan. Ned, upon arriving, fell in eagerly with her idea of going to Blackwood Hall.

"I hope the ghost appears for me too," he said, laughing, when Nancy had told him the story. "Say, how about going there by boat?"

"Wonderful."

After dinner Ned rented a trim little speedboat, and in a short time they reached an abandoned dock some distance from Blackwood Hall. A full moon shone down on the couple as they picked their way through the woods.

"Listen!" Nancy suddenly whispered.

From far away came the sound of chanting.

"It might be a séance!" Nancy said excitedly. "If we hurry, we may get there in time!"

Running ahead of Ned, Nancy paid scant heed to the ground underfoot, and stepped ankle-deep into a quagmire. When she tried to retreat, the mud tugged at her feet. Ned caught her by the arm.

"Stay back, Ned!" she cried out.

The warning came too late. Already Ned had followed her into the quagmire. He, too, tried to extricate himself without success.

"It's quicksand!" Ned cried hoarsely.

Inch by inch, he and Nancy felt themselves sinking lower and lower into the mire!

CHAPTER IX

Another Séance

REALIZING how serious their situation was, Ned urged Nancy to pull herself out of the quagmire by using him as a prop and jumping to firm ground.

"No, don't ask me to do that," Nancy replied. "I might save myself, but you would be pushed so far down, I couldn't possibly get help in time to pull you out."

"If you don't do it, we'll both lose our lives," Ned argued. "Hurry, Nancy! We're sinking fast!"

Nancy refused to listen to his pleas. Instead, she began to shout for help, hoping that some of the chanters would hear her. Ned, too, called loudly until his voice was hoarse.

No one came, and they kept sinking deeper into the quicksand. Soon Nancy was up to her chest.

"I'm afraid there's no help for us," Nancy said despairingly.

The youth scarcely heard her, for just then his feet struck something hard and firm.

"Nancy!" he cried. "I've hit bottom!"

Before she knew what was happening, he grasped her beneath the armpits and tugged hard. The muck gave a loud, sucking sound as it slowly and reluctantly released its hold. A few minutes later Nancy was safe and sound and on dry, firm ground, though she was plastered from heels to head with mud.

"You all right, Ned?"

"I'm okay," he answered.

Nancy scrambled to her feet. Now she must get Ned out! Desperately she looked around for something she could use to rescue him.

"Hold everything, Ned. I'll be back in a jiffy," Nancy called. She had remembered the long painter with which they had moored the motorboat to the dock.

Nancy raced through the darkness to the riverbank. She flicked on the lights of the small speedboat, untied the stout Manila rope which tied it to the pier, and a few minutes later was back at the edge of the quagmire where Ned was patiently waiting. She threw one end of the rope to the boy who calmly tied a noose under his arms. He directed her to toss the other end over the limb of a tree and then pull steadily.

Nancy struggled desperately to pull Ned from the quicksand. As the rope tightened, Ned began slowly but surely to emerge from the mire. Soon he was able to help with his arms and legs, and at last he succeeded in scrambling to safety beside Nancy.

For several minutes neither was able to speak, so exhausted were they from their violent efforts. As the two looked at each other, suddenly both Nancy and Ned began to laugh hysterically.

"If you could only see what you look like!" they exclaimed in the same breath.

Covered with mud and shaken by their unfortunate experience, their one desire was to get into clean clothes. The mystery, they decided, as they started back toward the dock, must wait for another time.

Later, at home once more and in dry clothes, Nancy began to wonder if Mrs. Putney had returned and whether she had been attending another séance. On a chance, she telephoned, but there was no answer. As Nancy reflected on her own adventure, she recalled the sound of chanting she and Ned had heard. Could it have come from Blackwood Hall? she wondered.

Immediately after breakfast the next morning, Nancy called at Mrs. Putney's home. The widow, looking very pale and tired, was wearing a dressing gown.

"I was up very late last night," she explained.

Nancy struggled to pull Ned from the quicksand

Then she added peevishly, "Why didn't you call me yesterday? It seems to me you're always away when I need you," Mrs. Putney grumbled. "Oh, dear! No one seems interested in my affairs—that is, no earthly being."

Nancy, though annoyed by the woman's attitude, was careful to hide her impatience. She realized that Mrs. Putney was a highly nervous individual, upset by the death of her husband, and recent events, and would have to be humored.

The widow remained stubbornly silent about telling where she had been the previous evening. Nancy, following a hunch, remarked:

"By the way, what were you chanting last night just before the séance?"

Mrs. Putney leaned forward in her chair, staring at Nancy as one stupefied. For a moment she looked as if she were going to faint. Then she recovered herself and whispered:

"Nancy Drew, how did you know where I was last evening?"

"Then it's true you were at a séance again last night?"

"Yes, Nancy. I tried to call you yesterday afternoon to let you know that I had been invited to another invocation of the spirits. But I couldn't reach you. *She* took me there again last night."

"She?"

"The woman in the veil," Mrs. Putney explained. "Yesterday afternoon I was instructed by telephone to go to Masonville and have dinner at the Claridge. Afterward, the car would be waiting for me. We drove somewhere into the country," the widow went on. "It seems strange, but I fell asleep again and didn't awaken until it was time to leave the car."

Nancy thought it very strange, indeed. Had the woman been drugged?

"As I opened my eyes, a long, opaque veil was draped over my head. I was led a short distance, where I was told there were several other persons who, like myself, were veiled."

"Did you learn their names?" Nancy interposed eagerly.

"Oh, no. My companion warned that to avoid annoying the spirits, we were not to speak to one another or ask questions."

"Then you all sang?" Nancy prompted as the widow stopped speaking.

"Yes, a woman led us in a prayerful chant," Mrs. Putney continued, her voice growing wistful at the recollection. "After a while we were taken indoors and the spirits came. They spoke to us through the control."

"How can you be certain it wasn't a trick?"

"Because my husband called me Addie. My first name is Adeline, you know, but he always liked Addie better. No one besides my husband ever called me by that name."

"Tricksters easily might have learned of it,"

Nancy pointed out. "The information could have been obtained from neighbors or relatives."

Apparently not listening, Mrs. Putney began to pace the floor nervously. "The spirits advised each of us to contribute money to carry on their earthly mission," she revealed.

"And what is that mission?"

The widow gave Nancy a quick look and replied, "We're supposed to turn money over to the earthly beings who make spiritual communication possible for us. Full instructions will be sent later. I gave them only fifty dollars last night. I felt I had to do that because everyone was giving something."

"A profitable night's work for those people!" Nancy remarked caustically. "You mustn't give another penny."

Mrs. Putney gave Nancy a cold stare. "Everything so far has seemed quite honest to me," she said.

Nancy was dismayed to realize that the widow was fast falling under the spell of the phonies who were trying to fleece her.

"Don't forget your jewelry was stolen," Nancy reminded her.

"I'm sure these people had nothing to do with that, Nancy."

"Mrs. Putney, at any time during the séance did you hear cries for help?"

"Why, no," the woman replied, startled. "Everything was very quiet." Then she added, "When the séance was over, I was taken outside again and helped into the car."

"Still veiled?"

"Oh, yes." A faraway look again came into her eyes. "You know, the trip home was like a dream. To tell the truth, I don't seem to remember anything about it. The next thing I really knew was that it was morning and I was lying on the divan in this very room."

Nancy was greatly disturbed at hearing this. It sounded too much like the strange actions of Lola and Sadie. She asked Mrs. Putney if she had been given anything to eat or drink before leaving the séance. The answer was No. She had noticed no unusual odors, either. Nancy was puzzled; somehow, the mediums must have brought on a kind of hypnotic sleep.

"Please don't ask me to give up the chance to get messages from my dear, departed husband," Mrs. Putney said, forestalling what Nancy was about to request.

Instead, on a sudden inspiration, Nancy told her to continue attending the séances, but asked to be kept informed of what happened. Pleased, Mrs. Putney promised, not realizing that Nancy hoped in this way to get evidence against the group. Then, at the proper moment, she would expose their trickery.

"I'll have to get busy before these people become suspicious and skip," Nancy said to herself as she drove home.

When Nancy told her father about the strange occurrences at Blackwood Hall, he agreed that the place should be thoroughly investigated to find out if fake séances were being carried on there.

"Nancy, I'm afraid to have you go near that place again," the lawyer said. "It sounds dangerous to me. Besides, we have no right to search anyone's property without a warrant. Perhaps your crowd of spirit-invoking fakers have rented the Humphrey mansion."

"But, Dad, everything depends upon it. Won't you go with me, and maybe Ned too?"

On the verge of refusing, Mr. Drew caught the eager, pleading look in his daughter's eyes. Also, he realized that they might very well make important discoveries at Blackwood Hall and the thought intrigued him.

"Tell you what!" he offered impulsively. "If Ned can go with us, we'll start out right after lunch! And I'll take care of the warrant. Captain McGinnis will fix me up."

Nancy ran to the telephone. "With both you and Ned to help me," she said excitedly, "that ghost is as good as trapped now!"

CHAPTER X

The Secret Door

SHORTLY after lunch Nancy arrived at Blackwood Hall with her father and Ned. What Nancy had counted on as a clue to fit into the puzzle, as she had worked it out in her mind, proved to be a disappointment.

"I was so sure there were going to be automobile tracks here," she said. "Mrs. Putney told me she was driven right to the door of the place where the séance was held."

"But here's something interesting," her father called from a spot among the trees.

As Nancy and Ned ran over, he pointed to several deep, narrow tracks and some footprints. The tracks looked as if they had been made by a wheelbarrow, which had been used to make several trips.

"I believe someone was busy moving things out of the house!" Mr. Drew exclaimed. "Anything valuable inside?"

"Furniture," Nancy replied. "Most of it would be too heavy to move by wheelbarrow, though."

"It's more likely the scamps carried away evidence which might incriminate them if found by the police," the lawyer said grimly. "Mediums' trappings, perhaps."

"Wonder if we can get inside," Ned said.

When he attempted to open the door, he found it locked. Thinking it might only be stuck, he and Mr. Drew heaved against the door with all their strength, and suddenly it gave way. The lock was broken.

"Not a very cheerful place," said Ned as the three stepped into the hallway. "This dim light would make anybody think he saw ghosts."

Nancy peered into the adjoining rooms. So far as a hasty glance revealed, none of the furniture had been disturbed. It was possible, of course, that the wheelbarrow tracks had no connection with the fake mediums at all, and perhaps Mrs. Putney's séances in turn had no connection with the ghost of Blackwood Hall!

"Let's separate and see what we can find out, anyway," Nancy proposed.

"All right," Mr. Drew agreed. "But call me, Nancy, if you come upon anything suspicious."

Eager to examine the organ again, Nancy walked along the hall and entered the huge room which was almost in complete darkness. Ned and her father began to search the other rooms.

With scarcely a thought that she was alone, Nancy went directly to the old organ, which stood at an angle across one corner. Laying down her lighted flashlight, she seated herself on the creaking bench and tried to play. No sound came forth.

"Why, that's funny!" Nancy thought, startled. She tried again, pumping the pedals and pressing the keys down firmly. "I certainly didn't dream I heard music coming from this organ! There must be a trick to it somewhere!"

Now deeply interested, Nancy began to examine the instrument inch by inch with her flashlight. There was a small space along the side wall, large enough for a person to squeeze behind. Peering in curiously, she was amazed to see a duplicate set of ivory keys at the rear of the organ!

"Why, the front of the organ is only a sham!"

Eager to investigate, Nancy pushed through the opening. There she found a low door in the wall of the room. "So this is how the ghost vanished so quickly!" she told herself.

Nancy tried the door, which was unlocked. Flashing her light, she saw that a flight of stairs led downward. Cautiously she began to descend. Only after proceeding a short distance along a damp, musty corridor did she regret that she had not summoned her father and Ned.

"They may wonder what's become of me," she thought. "I mustn't be gone long."

Intending to make a speedy inspection, Nancy quickened her steps along the corridor.

"This must be the secret tunnel the book mentioned!" she said to herself.

Soon Nancy came to a heavy walnut door, blocking the passageway. Her light revealed an iron bolt. As she slid it back and pushed the door open, she drew in her breath in sharp surprise. A strange green light on the floor of the room beyond illuminated the back of a ghostly figure standing just ahead of her!

Simultaneously, the flashlight was struck from her hand. It crashed on the floor and went out. The green light also faded away.

Fearful of a trap in the inky darkness, Nancy backed quickly into the corridor, slamming the heavy door and bolting it. Her heart pounding, she felt her way along the tunnel wall. Finally she stumbled up the stairway and through the exit behind the organ.

"Whew, that was a narrow escape!" she thought breathlessly. "I must find Dad and Ned."

Nancy hurried from room to room, upstairs and down, but did not see either of them. She was tempted to call out their names but then thought better of it. Very much concerned, Nancy decided that they must have left the house to investigate the grounds.

As she circled the mansion, the young detective tried to figure out under which room the secret tunnel had been built, and where it led. She noted that there was no outside exit from the cellar as most old houses had. Remembering the length of the musty underground corridor, she could very well believe that the exit was some distance from Blackwood Hall—perhaps in the woods.

When ten minutes or more had elapsed and neither Mr. Drew nor Ned had appeared, a harrowing thought began to disturb Nancy. Maybe the two of them were prisoners in the tunnel room! They might have found the outside entrance to the tunnel and been captured!

Frightened by this possibility, Nancy wondered what to do. Her first instinct was to go to the police. Then she realized that she could not drive the car to get help, because her father had the keys in his pocket. She finally decided that she would have to go back to the underground room at the end of the corridor alone and find out if her father and Ned were being held captive.

Forgetting any thought of safety for herself, she entered the house again. She ran to the organ room and squeezed through the opening to the secret door. There she closed her eyes for several seconds until they became accustomed to the darkness, then carefully she picked her way down the steps and along the passageway.

Reaching the heavy walnut door, she stooped down to look under the bottom for a light beyond. There was nothing but blackness.

Trying not to make any noise, Nancy slid the iron bolt and cautiously opened the door a crack. The place was dark. When nothing happened, Nancy decided to take a chance, and called out:

"Dad! Ned!"

There was no answer. Yet she thought possibly the two men might be lying gagged or unconscious not far away, and she could not see them. Without a light she had no way of finding out.

Nancy listened intently for several seconds, but heard only the sound of her own breathing.

"I'll have to get a light and come back here," she decided finally.

As Nancy was about to leave, she suddenly heard a scraping, creaking sound somewhere overhead.

"Maybe it's Dad or Ned!" Nancy thought excitedly.

Hopefully she hurried to the first floor. Seeing no one there, she climbed the front stairs to the second floor. As she reached the top step, Nancy froze to the spot.

At the far end of the hall, a wraithlike figure was just emerging from the far wall of the hallway!

CHAPTER XI

The Tunnel Room

NANCY uttered no sound. As she watched in the dim light, the ghost flitted noiselessly up a flight of stairs at the end of the hall which evidently led to the top floor.

Without thinking, Nancy started after it on tiptoe. Despite the heavy carpet, a floorboard groaned beneath her weight. Did she fancy that the filmy figure ahead hesitated a moment, then went on?

As she mounted the steps to the third floor Nancy heard another creaking sound. At the top she was just in time to see the white-draped figure again vanish into the wall!

The wall was solidly paneled with black walnut. Though Nancy searched carefully, running her fingers over every inch of the smooth wood panels, she could find no secret door or spring that might release a sliding partition. Returning to the second floor, she examined the panels there also, but without success.

Of one thing Nancy was convinced. The old house harbored more than one sinister character, how many she did not know. There was the figure at the organ, the one who had knocked her flashlight from her hand, the man who had scared Bess almost out of her wits, and now, the apparition she had followed up the stairs. Surely these could not all be one and the same "ghost."

"The one that went up the stairs was a live man or woman, I'm sure of that! But what was he up to?"

Knowing that a further investigation at this time would be worthless, Nancy started once more to look for her father and Ned.

After a futile search of the house and grounds, she decided:

"There's just a chance that they went back to the car and are waiting for me." She hurried down the road.

As she reached the place where the car had been parked, she halted in astonishment.

The automobile was gone!

Before she could examine the rutty road for tire prints, she heard the sound of hurrying footsteps. Whirling, she saw her father and Ned coming out of the woods.

"Nancy, thank heaven you're safe!" Ned exclaimed, hurrying to her side.

"But where's the car?" Nancy demanded.

"The car's been stolen!" Mr. Drew said grimly. "Ned and I heard voices outside and ran to investigate."

"Did you find out who it was?"

"No. But we caught a glimpse of a man streaking through the woods," Ned replied. "He was too far away for us to get a good look at him, and he gave us the slip."

"By the way, here's something I picked up near those wheelbarrow tracks that lead back through the woods," Mr. Drew remarked.

The lawyer handed Nancy a tubular piece of metal which appeared to have been taken from a collapsible rod such as magicians and fake mediums might use.

"Why, this piece is similar to the one I saw in the clearing the other day!" Nancy exclaimed.

"And look what I found on the kitchen stairway!" Ned exclaimed.

From his pocket he drew forth a miniature short-wave radio sending set.

"Does it work?" Mr. Drew asked eagerly.

"I'll see. Messages couldn't be sent very far with it, though."

"Could you tune it to send a message to the River Heights police station or a prowl car?"

Ned made some adjustments on the set, and began sending a request to the police asking that men be dispatched at once to Blackwood Hall. He gave the license number of the missing car and asked that it be rebroadcast over the police radio.

While they waited hopefully for action in response to Ned's call, Nancy related her adventures. She described the underground passageway, the strange appearance and disappearance of the "ghost," and the peculiar scraping sounds she had heard.

"If the police don't show up soon, we'll investigate the ghost room with my flashlight," Mr. Drew declared.

"Look!" Nancy cried out. "There's a car coming up the road."

The three quickly stepped behind some bushes and waited to see if they could identify the occupants of the approaching automobile before revealing their presence. To their relief, it was a State Police car.

"My message must have been relayed to them!" Ned exclaimed. "Swell!"

Two officers alighted, and the trio moved out of hiding to introduce themselves. Upon hearing the full details of what had happened, the troopers offered to make a thorough inspection of Blackwood Hall.

Nancy, Mr. Drew, and Ned accompanied them back to the mansion.

The police looked in every room but found no trace of its recent tenants. When they tackled the secret tunnel, Nancy stayed close behind, eager for a glimpse beyond the walnut door. It proved to be a tiny, empty room with no sign of a mysterious green light, a ghost or a human being. Furthermore, the room had no other exit.

"Is this little room under the house? Or is it located somewhere under the grounds?" Nancy asked one of the officers.

After making various measurements the men announced that it was located under the house, almost beneath the stairwell. It was not connected with the cellar, and no one could hazard a guess as to its original purpose.

"You may have thought you saw a ghost, but don't tell me anyone can get through a locked door," one officer chided the girl.

"I actually did see a figure in white," Nancy insisted quietly. "Something or someone knocked the flashlight from my hand. See, it's over there by the door."

In all fairness, Nancy could not blame the troopers for being a trifle skeptical. She almost began to doubt that she had ever had a frightening adventure in this spot.

Observing Nancy's crestfallen air, Mr. Drew said to the troopers, "Obviously this old house has been used by an unscrupulous gang. When they discovered we were here to check up on them, they moved out their belongings—my car as well."

"Stealing a car is a serious business," one officer commented. "We'll catch the thief, and when we do, we'll find out what has been going on in the old Humphrey house. Meanwhile, we'll have one of our men keep a close watch on this neck of the woods."

"No use sticking around here now," the other trooper added. "Whoever pulled the job has skipped."

"I'm going to keep working on this case until all the pieces in the puzzle can be made to fit together—even the ghosts!" Nancy told her father.

"Here's a bit of evidence," said the lawyer, taking the piece of telescopic rod from his pocket.

One trooper recognized it at once as magicians' or fake mediums' equipment, and asked for it to hand in with his report. Ned turned over the pocket radio sending set which had proved so valuable in bringing the police.

Though the license number of Mr. Drew's car had been broadcast over the police radio, there was no trace of it that night. The following afternoon Mr. Drew was notified that the car had been found abandoned in an adjacent state.

Accompanied by Nancy in her convertible, the lawyer traveled to Lake Jasper just across the state line. His automobile, found on a deserted road, had been towed to a local garage. Nothing had been damaged.

"Some people have no regard for other folks' property," the attendant remarked. "Probably a bunch o' kids helped themselves to your car to go joy riding."

But Nancy and her father were convinced that the car had not been "borrowed" by any joy riders. It had been used by a gangster to transport some unknown objects from Blackwood Hall!

What were the objects, and where had they been taken? Here was one more question to which Nancy must find the answer.

Nancy and her father had just returned home when Bess Marvin came bursting in. "Lola White has been talking wildly about you in her sleep!" Bess said ominously.

"What's so serious about that?" Nancy inquired.

"Lola's mother says she raves about a spirit warning her to have nothing more to do with Nancy Drew! If Lola does, the spirit will bring serious trouble to both of you!"

CHAPTER XII

Nancy's Plan

"LOLA believes that a spirit has warned her to have nothing more to do with me, or we'll both be harmed!" Nancy exclaimed.

"That's what she said," Bess answered. "I knew it would worry you."

Her face serious, Nancy started for the telephone. Bess ran after her.

"Are you going to call Mrs. White or Lola," she asked.

"No, I'll go to see them. But first I'm going to call Mrs. Putney." As Nancy looked for the telephone number in the directory, she added, "Members of a sinister ring of racketeers, posing as mediums are convinced that I'm on their trail. To protect themselves, they're having the so-called spirits warn their clients against me!"

"Do you think Mrs. Putney has been warned against you too?" Bess asked.

"We'll soon know." Nancy dialed the widow's number.

"Oh, Mrs. Putney, this is Nancy," the girl began. "I—"

A sharp click told her that Mrs. Putney had hung up. Nancy dialed again. Though the bell rang repeatedly at the other end of the line, there was no response.

"It's no use," she said at last, turning to Bess. "She refuses to talk to me. She must have been warned and is taking the warning seriously."

"What'll you do?"

"Let's go to her home," Nancy proposed. "This matter must be cleared up right away."

As the two girls arrived at the widow's home, they saw her picking flowers in the garden. But when she caught sight of the car, she turned and walked hastily indoors.

The girls went up the porch steps. They knocked and rang the doorbell. Finally they were forced to acknowledge that the woman had no intention of seeing them. Nancy was rather disturbed as she and Bess returned to the car.

"I'm afraid those swindlers have outsmarted us," she commented. "But not for long, I hope!"

She drove at once to the White home. Lola herself opened the door, but upon seeing Nancy, she backed away fearfully.

"You can't come in!" she said in a hoarse voice. "I never want to see you again."

"Lola, someone has poisoned you against me."

"The spirits have told me the truth about you, that's all. You're—you're an enemy of all of us."

Mrs. White, hearing the wild accusation, came to the door.

"Lola, what are you saying?" she said sternly. "Why haven't you invited our friends in?"

"Your friends—not mine!" the girl cried hysterically. "If you insist upon having them here, I'll leave!"

"Lola! How can you be so rude?"

Nancy was sorry to see Mrs. White berate her daughter for an attitude she felt was not entirely the girl's fault.

"I'll leave at once," Nancy said. "It's better that way."

"Indeed you must not," Mrs. White insisted.

"I think perhaps Lola has reached the point where she can work out her own affairs," Nancy said, but with a meaningful glance at Mrs. White, which the latter understood at once.

Nancy and Bess drove away, but pulled up just around the corner.

"I intend to keep watch on Lola," Nancy explained. "She may decide to act upon the suggestion that she straighten out her affairs herself."

"What do you think she'll do?" Bess asked.

"I'm not sure. But if she leaves the house, I'll trail her."

It became unpleasantly warm in the car, and Bess soon grew tired of waiting. Recalling that she had some errands to do, she presently decided to leave her friend.

Time dragged slowly for Nancy, who began to grow weary of the long vigil. Just as she was about to give up, she saw Lola come out of the house and hurry down the street.

Nancy waited until the girl was nearly out of sight before following slowly in the automobile. At the post office Nancy parked her car and followed Lola into the building where she watched her mail a letter.

"I'll bet she's written to those racketeers!" Nancy speculated.

Cruising along at a safe distance behind Lola, Nancy saw her board a bus, and followed it to the end of the line. There Lola waited a few minutes, then hopped an inbound bus, and returned home without having met anyone.

"Either she had an appointment with someone who didn't show up, or else she simply took the ride to think out her problems," Nancy decided.

Of one thing she was fairly certain. The old tree in the woods was no longer being used as a post office. Instead, the racketeers were instructing their clients to use the regular mails.

On a sudden impulse Nancy drove her car back to the post office to make a few inquiries. The clerk might remember a striking blonde like Lola. As she was approaching the General Delivery window, she saw a familiar figure speaking to the clerk. It was the woman that she and the girls had seen on the plane and who had followed them in New Orleans!

Darting behind a convenient pillar, Nancy heard the woman asking whether there were any letters for Mrs. Frank Immer.

The clerk left the window and soon returned shaking his head. The woman thanked him, then left the building. When Nancy was sure the coast was clear she followed. Starting her car, Nancy kept a safe distance behind the woman. A few minutes later she saw her quarry disappear into the Claymore Hotel.

Nancy drove around the hotel once or twice, looking for a place to park. It was some time later that she approached the hotel clerk's desk. Examination of the register revealed no guest by the name of Mrs. Frank Immer, nor had anyone signed in from Louisiana.

"But I saw Mrs. Immer enter here," insisted Nancy. "She wore a large black hat and a blue dress."

The clerk turned to the cashier and asked if he had seen anyone answering the description.

"Maybe you mean Mrs. Frank Egan," the cashier volunteered. "She just checked out."

"How long ago?"

"About ten minutes."

The cashier could not tell Nancy where the woman had gone, for she had left no forwarding address. From a bellhop she learned that Mrs. Egan had directed a taxi to take her to the airport.

"She said something about going to Chicago," the boy recalled.

"Thanks." Nancy smiled.

Determined that Mrs. Egan should not leave the city without at least answering a few questions, Nancy sped to the airport. To her bitter disappointment, as Nancy pulled up, a big airliner took off gracefully from the runway.

"Mrs. Egan probably is aboard!" she groaned.

Nancy checked and confirmed that a woman answering the description had bought a ticket for Chicago, in the name of Mrs. Floyd Pepper.

"My one chance now of having her questioned or trailed is to wire the Chicago police!" Nancy decided. "I'll ask Dad to make the request."

She telephoned to explain matters, and Mr. Drew agreed to send a telegram at once.

Nancy, having done all she could in the matter, returned to the Claymore Hotel with a new plan in mind. She asked for some stationery with the

Claymore letterhead. When she arrived home her father was there.

"Dad, I want to find out if Mrs. Egan has any part in the séances, the stock deals, or the money that used to be put in the walnut tree," said Nancy. "Will you tell me honestly what you think of this plan? I'm going to type notes to Mrs. Putney, Lola White, and Sadie Green."

"Using Mrs. Egan's name?"

"That's the idea. If it doesn't work, then I'll try the name of Immer later. I won't try imitating Mrs. Egan's signature in the hotel register. I'll just type the name."

"But what can you say without giving yourself away?" asked Mr. Drew.

"I'll write that my plans have been changed suddenly," Nancy said. "I'll request them to send all communications to Mrs. Hilda Egan at the Claymore Hotel."

"When she isn't there? And why Hilda? Isn't the name Mrs. Frank Egan?"

"That's how I'll know the answers belong to *me*. I doubt if her clients know her first name, anyway."

Mr. Drew chuckled. "Anyone could tell that you have legal blood in your veins," he said. "But aren't you forgetting one little detail?"

"What's that?" Nancy asked in surprise.

"If Mrs. Putney, Sadie, Lola, or any of the others have ever had any correspondence with Mrs.

Egan, they'll be suspicious of the letters. They may question a typed name instead of one written in her own hand."

"How would it be," said Nancy, "if in the corner of the envelope, I draw the insigne of the Three Branch Ranch!"

"Well, here's hoping," said Mr. Drew a trifle dubiously.

Later that day Nancy wrote the letters, then rushed over to the Claymore and persuaded the hotel clerk, who knew her to be an amateur detective, to agree to turn over to her any replies which might come addressed to Mrs. Hilda Egan.

"Since you say these letters will be in answer to letters you yourself have written, I'll do it," he agreed.

All the next day Nancy waited impatiently for word from the Chicago police in reply to her father's telegram. None came, nor did she receive a call from the clerk at the Claymore Hotel.

"Maybe my idea wasn't so good after all," she thought.

But on the second day, the telephone rang. Nancy's pulse hammered as she recognized the voice of the Claymore Hotel clerk.

"Nancy Drew?"

"Yes. Have you any mail for me?"

"A letter you may want to pick up is here," he said hurriedly.

CHAPTER XIII

Complications

THE letter awaiting Nancy at the Claymore Hotel proved to be from Sadie Green, the girl who worked at the Lovelee Cosmetic Company.

In the communication, which the girl never dreamed would be read by anyone except Mrs. Egan, she revealed she had received a bonus and would gladly donate it to the poor orphans cared for at the Three Branch Home.

". . . In accordance with messages from their deceased parents," the letter ended.

"So that's what they are up to!" Nancy thought grimly. "There's no greater appeal than that of poor, starving orphans! The very idea of trying to rob hard-working girls with such hocus-pocus!"

As soon as Nancy returned home, she promptly typed a reply on the hotel stationery warning Sadie that since certain unscrupulous persons were endeavoring to turn a legitimate charity into a racket, she was to pay no attention to any writ-

ten or telephoned messages, unless they came from Mrs. Egan herself at the Claymore Hotel.

Nancy's next move was made only after she had again consulted her father. At first he was a little reluctant to consent to the daring plan she proposed, but when she outlined its possibilities, he agreed to help her.

"Write down the address of this shop in Winchester," he said, scribbling it on a paper. "Unless I'm mistaken, you can buy everything you need there."

As a result of Nancy's talk with her father and also with Ned Nickerson, another letter went forward to Sadie Green. The note merely said that the girl would be required to attend an important séance the following night. She was instructed to wait for a car at Cross and Lexington streets.

At the appointed hour, Nancy, heavily veiled, rode beside her father in the front seat of a car borrowed from a friend. In order not to be recognized, Mr. Drew had a felt hat pulled low over his eyes.

"Dad, you look like a second-story man!" Nancy teased him as they parked at the intersection. "Do you think Sadie will show up?"

"I see a blond girl coming now," he replied.

Nancy turned her head slightly and recognized Sadie. Making a slow gesture with her gloved hand, she motioned the girl into the back seat. Mr. Drew promptly pulled away from the curb.

The automobile took a direct route to the vicinity of Blackwood Hall. Nancy covertly watched Sadie from beneath her veil. The girl was very nervous and kept twisting her handkerchief as they approached. But when they got out and started walking, she gave no sign that the area was familiar.

Ned Nickerson had followed in another borrowed automobile which he concealed in a clump of bushes. Then he removed a small suitcase from the trunk, and started off through the woods.

Meanwhile, Nancy and Sadie, with Mr. Drew a little distance behind, approached Blackwood Hall.

"I hope everything goes through as planned," Nancy thought with a twinge of uneasiness. "If Ned is late getting here—"

Just then she saw a faint, greenish light glowing weirdly through the trees directly ahead. At the same moment came a strange, husky chant.

Nancy stepped to one side so that Sadie might precede her on the path. The girl gazed at the green point of light as one hypnotized.

"The spirit speaks!" Nancy intoned.

Simultaneously a luminous hand seemed to appear out of nowhere. It floated, unattached, and reached out as if to touch Sadie.

"My child," intoned an old man's cracked voice, "I am your beloved grandfather on your dear mother's side."

"Not Elias Perkins!" Sadie murmured in awe.

"The spirit of none other, my child. Sadie, I have been watching you and I am worried—most sorely worried. You must give no more money to the Three Branch Ranch or to any cause which my spirit cannot recommend."

"But, Grandfather—"

"Furthermore," continued the cracked voice, taking no note of the interruption, "follow no orders or directions from anyone, unless that person writes or speaks his name backward. Mind this well, Sadie, my child, for it is important."

The voice gradually drifted away as the green light began to grow dim. Soon there was only darkness and deep silence in the woods.

"Oh, Grandfather! Come back! Speak to me again!" Sadie pleaded.

"The séance is concluded," Nancy murmured.

She took Sadie by the arm and led her back to the waiting car. All the way home Sadie remained silent. Only once did she speak and that was to ask "the veiled lady" the meaning of the strange instructions issued by her grandfather.

Nancy spoke slowly and in a low monotone, "You are to reveal no information to anyone and take no orders from anyone unless he spells or speaks his or her name backward."

"I don't understand," Sadie said.

"There are unscrupulous people who seek to

take advantage of you. Your grandfather's spirit is trying to protect you. He has given you a means of identifying the good and the evil. You have been in communication with a Mrs. Egan, have you not?"

The blond girl nodded. And Nancy continued, "Should Mrs. Egan approach you again, saying 'I am Mrs. Egan,' then beware! But should she say 'I am Mrs. Nage,' then you will know that she is to be trusted, even as you trust the spirit of Elias Perkins."

"Oh! I see now what Grandfather meant," Sadie said, and became silent again.

At Cross and Lexington streets, the girl left the car. Nancy and her father drove on home, to find Ned awaiting them.

"How did I do?" the youth demanded in the cracked voice of Elias Perkins as they entered the house together.

Nancy chuckled. "A perfect performance!"

"You don't know the half of it," Ned joked. "I almost messed up the whole show."

As the three enjoyed milk and sandwiches in the Drew kitchen, the young man revealed that he had nearly lost the hand from the end of the rod.

"Next time you want me to perform, buy a better grade of equipment!" He laughed, biting into another ham sandwich.

Ned was referring to the props used during the séance, which Nancy had purchased earlier that day at a store in Winchester. These included a telescopic reaching rod, and the luminous wax hand, as well as a bottle of phosphorus and olive oil, guaranteed to produce a ghostly effect when the cork was removed, which would disappear again at the required moment when it was stoppered.

"When I took the bottle from the suitcase, I nearly dropped it," Ned confessed. "And what's a séance in the dark worth without a spooky light?" he added, laughing.

On the following day, Nancy called at Sadie's home. Sadie was at work, but elderly Mr. Green, eager for companionship, told Nancy everything she wished to know.

"That granddaughter o' mine ain't so foolish as I was afeared," he said promptly. "This morning she says to me 'Grandpa, I've made up my mind to save my money and not give it away to every Tom, Dick, and Harry who asks me for it.' What do you think o' that?"

"Splendid!" Nancy approved. "I hoped Sadie would have a change of heart."

To test Sadie further, Nancy asked Ned the next day to telephone the girl at the Lovelee Cosmetic Company.

"I want to prove a couple of things," she said.

"First of all, I want to find out whether Sadie is really following my instructions, and second, if she knows the name of Howard Brex."

Ned began to laugh. "How would you pronounce Brex backward?"

Nancy smiled too. "Guess you'll have to use his first name. 'Drawoh' is easy."

While Nancy listened on an extension at the Drew home, Ned made the call. He addressed the girl as Eidas instead of Sadie and added, "This is Drawoh speaking."

"My name ain't Eidas, and I don't know what you're talking about," the girl retorted, failing to understand.

Ned quickly asked her to think hard. Suddenly Sadie said:

"Oh, yes, I remember. And what did you say your name is?"

"Drawoh."

After a moment's reflection, the girl said, "I guess I don't know you."

"No," said Ned. "But tell me, have you had any recent communications asking you for money?"

"One came today, but I threw it away," Sadie replied. "I'm not giving any more of my money to those folks. I have to go now."

Sadie hung up.

"Good work, Nancy!" Ned declared as he rejoined her. "Apparently that trick séance brought Sadie to her senses."

"For a few days, anyhow," Nancy agreed. "The job isn't over, though, until these swindlers are behind bars! They still have great influence over Lola and Mrs. Putney and goodness knows how many other people.

"I can easily understand how a person like Sadie would be so gullible, but it's almost unthinkable that Mrs. Putney would fall for that stuff," Ned said.

While the two friends were talking, Hannah Gruen called Nancy to the telephone. The message was from the clerk at the Claymore Hotel. The late-morning mail had brought two more letters addressed to Mrs. Egan.

"Isn't that wonderful, Ned?" Nancy cried. "I'll have to go over to the hotel right away."

"I'll take you there," Ned offered.

He drove Nancy to the hotel and waited in the car while she went inside. The girl was gone several minutes. When she returned, her face was downcast, and she looked very disturbed.

"What's the matter?" Ned demanded. "Didn't you get the letters?"

Nancy shook her head. "The regular clerk went to lunch," she explained. "In his absence, another clerk gave the letters to someone else!"

CHAPTER XIV

The Cabin in the Woods

"A young woman picked up the letters," Nancy told Ned. "Mrs. Egan must have discovered our scheme and sent a messenger. She was lucky enough, or else she planned it that way, to have the letters called for when my friend was off duty."

"Maybe Mrs. Egan's back in town," Ned suggested.

"Yes, that's possible. The police were never able to trace her. According to word Dad received, she left the plane at one of the stops between here and Chicago."

Ned whistled softly. "Wow! If she's back here, she'll be in your hair, Nancy!"

"She hasn't registered at the Claymore. I found that out. But that doesn't prove she isn't in River Heights. Ned, something's got to break in this case soon. We know that there are several people in the racket and it may be that Brex is the mastermind behind everything. Blackwood Hall evidently had been used as headquarters until we got too interested for their comfort. All of the supernatural hocus-pocus was used not only to fleece gullible victims, but also to scare us off the scent. I feel that there will be a showdown within the next few days."

"Well, I want to be there when that happens, Nancy," said Ned.

Later that day, Nancy called George and Bess and asked them to go with her to Blackwood Hall. The drive to the river road was uneventful. They parked their car some distance away and all three trekked through the walnut woods in the direction of the historic mansion.

"But, Nancy, what *do* you expect to find this time?" asked Bess.

"I realized when I was reviewing the case with Ned today that we never had checked those wheelbarrow tracks from Blackwood Hall. They may lead us to the spot where the gang is now making its headquarters."

The old house looked completely abandoned as the girls approached.

Suddenly George cried, "The wheelbarrow tracks lead away from the house and right into the woods."

For some distance the girls tramped on, stopping now and then to examine footprints where the ground was soft. Suddenly, in the flickering sunlight ahead, they caught sight of a cabin in a clearing among the trees. Approaching cautiously they noted that all the windows were covered with black cloths on the inside. The wheelbarrow tracks led to what obviously was the back door.

"That must be the place!" Nancy whispered excitedly. "See! A road leads right up to the front door just as Mrs. Putney told me!"

Bess began to back away, tugging at George's sleeve. "Let the troopers find out!" she pleaded.

Nancy and George moved stealthily forward without her. After circling and seeing no signs of life around the place, George boldly knocked several times on the front door.

"Deserted," she observed. "We may as well leave."

Nancy gazed curiously at the curving road which led from the cabin. Only a short stretch was visible before it lost itself in the walnut woods.

"Let's follow the road," she proposed. "I'm curious to learn where it comes out."

Bess, however, would have no part of the plan. She pointed out that already they were over a mile from Nancy's car.

"And if we don't get back soon, it may be stolen, just as your father's was," she added.

This remark persuaded Nancy reluctantly to give up her plan. The girls trudged back through the woods to the other road. The car was where they had left it.

"I have an idea!" Nancy declared as they started off. "Why don't we try to drive to the cabin?"

Nancy was convinced that by following the main road they might come to a side lane which would lead them to the cabin. Accordingly, they drove along the designated highway, carefully scrutinizing the sides for any private road whose entrance might have been camouflaged.

"I see a side road!" Bess suddenly cried out.

Nancy, who had noticed the narrow dirt road at the same instant, turned into it.

"Wait!" George directed. "Another one branches off just a few yards ahead on the highway we were following. That may be the one instead of this."

Uncertain, Nancy stopped the car and idled the engine. Before the girls could decide which road to follow, an automobile sped past on the highway they had left only a moment before. Nancy and the others caught a fleeting glimpse of a heavily veiled woman at the wheel. On the rear seat they thought they saw a reclining figure.

The car turned into the next narrow road, and then disappeared.

"Was that Mrs. Putney on the back seat?" George asked, highly excited.

"I didn't get a good enough look to be sure," Nancy replied. "I got the car license number, though. Let me write it down before I forget."

"Hurry!" George urged as Nancy wrote the

numbers on a pad from her purse. "We have to follow that car!"

"But not too close," Nancy replied. "We'd make them suspicious."

The girls waited three minutes before backing out into the main highway and then turning into the adjacent road. Though the automobile ahead had disappeared, tire prints were plainly visible.

The road twisted through a stretch of woodland. When finally the tire prints turned off into a heavily wooded narrow lane, Nancy was sure they were not far from the cabin. She parked among some trees and they went forward on foot.

"There it is!" whispered Nancy, recognizing the chimney. "Bess, I want you to take my car, drive to River Heights, and look up the name of the owner of the car we just saw. Here's the license number.

"After you've been to the Motor Vehicle Bureau, please phone Mrs. Putney's house. If she answers, we'll know it wasn't she we saw in the car. Then get hold of Dad or Ned, and bring one of them here as fast as you can. We may need help. Got it straight?"

"I—I—g-guess so," Bess answered.

"Hurry back! No telling what may happen while you're away."

The two watched as Nancy's car rounded a bend and was lost to view.

Then Nancy and George walked swiftly through the woods toward the cabin. Approaching the building, Nancy and George were amazed to find that no car was parked on the road in front.

"How do you figure it?" George whispered as the girls crouched behind bushes. "We certainly saw tire marks leading into this road!"

"Yes, but the car that passed may have gone on without stopping. Possibly the driver saw us and changed her plans. Wait here, and watch the cabin while I check the tire marks out at the end of the road."

"All right. But hurry. If anything breaks here, I don't want to be alone."

From the bushes George saw Nancy hurry down the road and out of sight around a bend.

For some time everything was quiet. Suddenly George's attention was drawn to a wisp of smoke from the wide stone chimney.

"There's someone in there, that's sure," she concluded. "Somebody's lighted a fire."

Overpowering curiosity urged George to find out what was going on inside the cabin. She could see nothing through the black-draped windows. Trying to decide whether to wait for Nancy or to make some move of her own, she noticed smoke seeping through the cracks around the door!

"The place must be on fire!" George exclaimed. When still no sound came from inside, she could stand the strain no longer. "I'm going to break in!" she decided.

She flung herself against the locked door, but it scarcely budged. Looking about, she found a rock the size of a baseball. She let it fly at the window nearest the door. The glass splintered and the stone carried with it the black curtain that had covered the window. With a stick she poked out the jagged bits of glass that still clung to the pane. When the smoke had cleared, George stuck her head through the opening.

The one-room interior was deserted, and *there was no fire,* not even in the big stone fireplace! A few wisps of smoke remained. But it did not smell like wood smoke.

"I didn't dream up that smoke," George thought, growing more uneasy all the time. "But the door was locked and I saw no one leave."

Time dragged on, and still Nancy did not return. Finally, after an hour had elapsed, George, alarmed, tramped back to the road where they had taken leave of Bess.

She was about to start for River Heights on foot when the convertible came into view around a bend. Bess pulled alongside.

"Do you know anything about Nancy?" George asked quickly.

"Why, no."

Her cousin related the strange story of the

George hurled a rock at the window

cabin and Nancy's disappearance. Bess, too, was greatly concerned.

"And I didn't bring anyone along, either," she wailed. "Mr. Drew was called out of town unexpectedly, and I couldn't find Ned."

"Just when we need them so desperately! Did you find the car owner's name?"

"Yes, it belongs to Mrs. Putney! But what are we going to do about Nancy?"

"I think Mr. Drew should be notified if we can possibly get word to him. Hannah may know where to reach him by telephone," said George.

The girls made a hurried trip to the Drew home. The housekeeper told them that the lawyer had departed in great haste and was to send word later where he could be reached.

"I really don't know what to do," Hannah Gruen said anxiously. "The Claymore Hotel has been trying to get in touch with Nancy, too. The chief clerk there wants to see her right away. We'd better notify the police. I dislike doing it, though, until we've tried everything else."

No one had paid the slightest attention to Togo, who was lying on his own special rug in the living room. Now, as if understanding the housekeeper's remark, he began to whine.

"What's the matter, old boy?" George asked, stooping to pat the dog. "Are you trying to tell us something about Nancy?"

Togo gave two sharp yips.

"Say! Do you suppose Togo could pick up Nancy's trail and lead us to her?" George asked.

"When she's around the neighborhood, he finds her in a flash," Hannah Gruen said. "Nancy can scarcely go a block without his running after her, if he can get loose."

"Then why don't we give him a chance now?" Bess urged. "Maybe if you get something of Nancy's, a shoe, perhaps, he might pick up the scent—"

"It's worth trying," the housekeeper said, starting for the stairway.

She returned in a few moments with one of Nancy's tennis shoes, and announced she was going along on the search. Taking the eager Togo with them, the group drove back to the spot where Nancy was going to investigate the tire marks. George dropped the shoe in the dust.

"Go find Nancy, Togo!" Bess urged. "Find her!"

Togo whined and sniffed at the shoe. Then, picking it up in his teeth, he ran down the road.

"Oh, he thinks we are playing a game," Mrs. Gruen said in disappointment. "This isn't going to work."

"No, Togo knows what he is doing," George insisted, for in a moment he was back.

Dropping the shoe, the dog began to sniff the

ground excitedly. Then he trotted across the road and into the woods, the others following. Reaching a big walnut tree, he circled it and began to bark.

"But Nancy isn't here!" quavered Bess.

Suddenly the little dog struck off for some underbrush and began barking excitedly.

CHAPTER XV

Two Disappearances

"Togo's found something!" Bess exclaimed, following George, who was parting the bushes that separated them from the dog.

George uttered a startled exclamation as she came upon Nancy stretched out on the ground only a few feet away. Togo was licking his mistress's face as if begging her to regain consciousness.

Just as Hannah Gruen reached the spot, Nancy stirred and sat up. Seeing her dog, she reached over in a dazed sort of way to pat him.

"Hello, Togo," she mumbled. "Who— *How* did you get here? Where am I?" Then, seeing her friends, she smiled wanly.

Observing that she had no serious injuries, they pressed her for an explanation.

"I don't know what happened," Nancy admitted.

On the ground near the spot where the cabin road crossed another dirt road, she had found the familiar Three Branch insigne.

This time, a tiny arrow had been added. Without stopping to summon George, Nancy had hurried along the trail until she came upon another arrow.

A series of arrows had led her deeper into the woods. Finally she had come to a walnut tree nearly as large as the famous Humphrey Walnut.

The tree had a small hollow space in its trunk. It contained no message, however. She had been about to turn back when a piece of paper on the ground had caught her eye. Examination had revealed that it was a half sheet torn from a catalog.

"It matched that scrap of paper I found in the clearing near the Humphrey Walnut," Nancy said.

Obviously the sheet had been ripped from the catalog of a supply house for magicians' equipment. One advertisement offered spirit smoke for sale.

While Nancy had been reading, she had heard footsteps and looked up. Through the woods, some distance up the path, she had seen a young woman approaching. Hastily Nancy stepped back, intending to hide behind the walnut tree.

At that moment something had struck her from behind.

"That's the last I remember," she added ruefully.

"Who would do such a wicked thing?" Mrs. Gruen demanded in horror.

"It's easy to guess," Nancy replied. "The tree must be another place where the members of the gang collect money from their victims. I probably had the bad luck to arrive here at the moment a client was expected.

"You mean the same fellow who had the reaching rod hit you to get you out of the way?" Bess asked. "Oh," she added nervously, "he still may be around!"

"I doubt it," Nancy said. "He probably took the money that girl left, and ran."

"I'm going to inform the police!" Hannah Gruen announced in a determined voice.

Nancy tried to dissuade her, but for once her arguments had no effect. On the way home with the girls, Mrs. Gruen herself stopped at the office of the State Police. She revealed all she knew of the attack upon Nancy.

As a result, troopers searched the woods thoroughly; but, exactly as Nancy had foreseen, not a trace was found of her assailant. However, when they searched the interior of the cabin, they found evidence pointing to the fact that its recent residents were interested in magic.

When they reached home, Mrs. Gruen told Nancy about the telephone call from a clerk at the

Claymore Hotel. She went to see him at once, and was given a letter addressed to Mrs. Egan. It was signed by Mrs. Putney!

The note merely said that the services of Mrs. Egan would no longer be required. The spirit of Mrs. Putney's departed husband was again making visitations to his former home to advise her.

Taking the letter with her, Nancy mulled over the matter for some time.

The next morning, she decided to pay Mrs. Putney a visit, hoping she would be able to see her this time. But Mrs. Putney was not there, and a neighbor in the next house told Nancy she had been gone all morning.

"Doesn't Mrs. Putney ever drive her car?" Nancy asked, seeing it through a garage window.

"Not since her husband died."

"Does she have someone else drive her?"

"Oh, no! She won't let a soul touch the car."

Nancy was puzzled. Someone must have taken the car without Mrs. Putney's permission.

"If that woman we saw in the back seat was Mrs. Putney, maybe she didn't know where she was or what she was doing, any more than poor Lola did when she walked into the river!" Nancy told herself.

Nancy thanked the woman and withdrew. She hurried back to the garage to look for evidence that the car had been used recently. Fortunately the door was not locked. She examined the car carefully. It was covered with a film of dust and the rear axle was mounted on jacks. It had obviously not been driven for some time.

Something else struck Nancy as peculiar. The license plate bore a number that was different from the one registered as Mrs. Putney's.

"Hers must have been stolen and someone else's plate put on her car!" the young detective thought excitedly. "Maybe this number belongs to one of the racketeers and he used Mrs. Putney's to keep people from tracing him!"

Nancy dashed off in her convertible to the Motor Vehicle Bureau office. There she learned that the license on the widow's car had been issued to a Jack Sampson in Winchester, fifty miles from River Heights. But this revelation was mild in comparison with what the clerk told her next.

"Jack Sampson died a few months ago. His car was kept in a public garage. The executor of the estate reported that the license plate had been stolen."

As soon as Nancy recovered from her astonishment, she thanked the clerk for the information. Telephone calls to Winchester brought out the fact that the deceased man's reputation had been above reproach. He could not have been one of the racketeers. Nancy decided that before telling the police where the stolen license plates could be found, she would give Mrs. Putney a chance to tell what she knew about it all.

Hurrying back, she was just in time to see the widow coming up the street with several packages. Nancy hastened to her side and offered to take them. Although Mrs. Putney allowed her to carry them, she did not invite Nancy into the house. Therefore, Nancy told her story of the license plate as they stood on the front porch.

"I wasn't in that car you saw, and you must be mistaken about the license plate," Mrs. Putney told her flatly.

"Come, I'll show you," Nancy urged, leading the way to the garage and opening the door. "Why—why—" she gasped in utter bewilderment.

The correct license number was back on the car!

"You see why I have come to doubt your ability to help me," Mrs. Putney said coldly. "I no longer need your assistance, Nancy. As a matter of fact, I have every expectation of getting my stolen jewelry back very soon. My husband's spirit has been visiting me right here at home as he used to do, and he assures me that everything will turn out satisfactorily."

Leaving Nancy distressed and more concerned than ever, Mrs. Putney walked into the house without even saying good-by. As Nancy started away, she decided that further protection for the widow would have to come from the police.

Next, she drove to police headquarters to see her old friend Captain McGinnis. Nancy explained that she knew someone had appropriated the Putney license plate, and probably would do so again.

"Mrs. Putney has told me some things that make me think someone prowls around there late at night or early in the morning," Nancy told him. "I'm afraid she may be in danger."

Nancy kept to herself the idea that a member of the ring of fake mediums might be playing the role of Mr. Putney's spirit. She had noticed that two windows of Mrs. Putney's bedroom opened onto the roof of a porch. It would be very easy for an agile man to climb up there and perform as the late Mr. Putney.

The officer agreed to keep men on duty to watch the house night and day. Nancy was so hopeful of rapid developments, now, that every time the telephone rang, she was sure it was word that the police had caught one or more of the gang.

But when she had received no word for a whole day, she went to see Captain McGinnis. He told her that plainclothesmen had kept faithful watch of the Putney home, but reported that no one had been found trying to break in; in fact, Captain

McGinnis said he was thinking of taking the detectives off the case because the house was now unoccupied.

"You mean Mrs. Putney has gone away?" Nancy asked incredulously.

"Yes, just this morning," the officer replied. "Bag and baggage. Probably gone on a vacation."

Nancy was amazed to hear this, and also chagrined. She had not expected such a turn of events!

"I'm certain Mrs. Putney isn't on vacation," Nancy told herself grimly. "It's more likely that she received a spirit message advising her to leave.

Recalling the widow's mention of getting back the stolen jewelry, Nancy surmised that Mrs. Putney might have gone off on some ill-advised errand to recover it. Thoroughly discouraged, Nancy had yet another disappointment to face. Scarcely had she reached home, when an urgent telephone call came from Mrs. White.

"Oh, Nancy! The very worst has happened!" the woman revealed tearfully. "Lola's gone!"

"Gone? Where, Mrs. White?"

"I don't know," Lola's mother wailed. "She left a note saying she was leaving home. Oh, Nancy, you must help me find her!"

CHAPTER XVI

A Well-Baited Trap

WORRIED over the news about Lola, Nancy went
without delay to see Mrs. White. She learned that
the girl had departed very suddenly. Mrs. White
was convinced her daughter had been kidnapped
or had met with foul play.

"Have no fear on that score," Nancy said reas-
suringly. She told Mrs. White of her idea that a
group of clever thieves might be mesmerizing or
threatening their victims in order to get their
money. "They're too interested in Lola's earnings
to let anything happen to her," she finished.

After telling Mrs. White she was sure her
daughter would realize her mistake and return
home, Nancy left. She decided to walk in the park
and thrash matters out in her own mind. Presently she seated herself on a bench and absently
watched two swans in a nearby pond.

She scarcely noticed when a thin woman in

133

black sat down beside her. But when the stranger took out a handkerchief and wiped away tears, Nancy suddenly became attentive.

"Are you troubled?" she inquired kindly.

"Yes," the woman answered. Eager to confide in someone, she began to pour out her story.

"It's my daughter." The stranger sighed. "She's causing me so much worry. Nellie works and makes good money, but lately all she does is complain she hasn't a penny. She must be frittering it away on worthless amusements."

Nancy listened attentively, made a few queries, and then suggested to the woman that she ask her daughter if she made a practice of leaving money in a certain black walnut tree.

"In a walnut tree!" exclaimed the woman.

"Also, find out if she sends money through the mail, and if so, to whom," Nancy instructed. "Ask her if she ever visits a medium or is helping support orphans at a place called Three Branch Home. Find out if you can whether or not spirits mysteriously appear to her at night."

"My goodness!" the woman cried in amazement. "You must be a policewoman!"

Nancy scribbled her father's unlisted telephone number on a scrap of paper and gave it to the stranger. "If you need help or have any information, call me here at once," she added.

The woman pocketed the telephone number

and quickly rose from the bench. "Thank you, miss. Thank you kindly," she murmured.

Only after the stranger had disappeared, did it occur to Nancy that she might have been unwise in offering advice so freely.

Definitely annoyed at herself, Nancy returned home, where she found a telegram from her father. It said that private detectives working for him in Chicago had traced some of Mrs. Putney's stolen jewelry to a pawnshop there. But the ring belonging to her husband and her pearl necklace were still missing.

Her father's mention of the Putney jewels caused Nancy to wonder anxiously what had become of the widow and of Lola White. Could there be any connection in their simultaneous disappearance? A panicky thought struck the young detective. Perhaps they were being held prisoners at some hideout of the racketeers.

Almost at once Nancy put this idea out of her mind. These people were too clever to resort to kidnapping. Since they knew that Blackwood Hall was under surveillance, it was logical to assume that the gang was operating in new surroundings. If she could discover where Mrs. Putney had gone, then perhaps she would be able to locate the men who were seeking to separate the gullible woman from her money.

From Mrs. Putney's next-door neighbor Nancy

learned that her late husband had owned a hunting lodge on Lake Jasper, across the state line, where he had spent a great deal of time each summer.

So far as anyone knew, his widow had not visited the place since his death. Nancy thought there was a good possibility that Mrs. Putney might be at the lodge now. Moreover, Lake Jasper was the place where Mr. Drew's stolen car had been found!

Hannah Gruen did not entirely approve of Nancy's making a trip to Lake Jasper, preferring that she wait until her father returned. In the end, the housekeeper agreed to the plan but only after the parents of Bess and George had consented to having their daughters accompany Nancy.

"If for any reason you decide to stay more than one night, telephone me at once," Hannah begged.

Taking only light luggage, the girls started off early the next morning. During the drive, Nancy confided to her friends that she suspected Lola had run away from home and did not intend to return.

"Those people who seem to have her in their control have probably found her a job in another town. I must do everything I can to trace her, as soon as I find out about Mrs. Putney."

Lake Jasper was situated in the heart of pine woods country, and was one of a dozen beautiful small lakes in the area. Not knowing Mrs. Putney's address, the girls obtained directions at the post office. They learned that the hunting lodge was at the head of the lake, in an isolated spot.

"No sense going there until we've had lunch," remarked Bess. "It's after one o'clock now, and I'm faint from hunger."

At an attractive tearoom nearby, the girls enjoyed a delicious lake-trout dinner. Later, as they walked toward the car, Nancy suddenly halted.

"Girls," she said, "do my eyes deceive me, or is that Lola White walking ahead of us?"

The person Nancy pointed out was some distance down the street, her back to the three girls.

"It's Lola all right!" Bess agreed. "What do you suppose she's doing at Lake Jasper?"

"My guess is she's here with Mrs. Putney," Nancy replied grimly.

"But I'm sure they don't know each other," Bess said.

"Perhaps the gang arranged for her to come up here with Mrs. Putney," Nancy suggested.

The girls drove half a block ahead of Lola. Satisfied that they had made no mistake in identifying the girl, they alighted and walked directly toward her.

At an intersection the four met. Lola gazed at them, but her face was expressionless. She passed the trio without a sign of recognition.

"Well, of all things!" said Bess as the three

friends halted to stare after Lola. "She certainly was pretending she didn't know us."

"Maybe she didn't," Nancy replied. "Lola acted as she did the time Ned and I found her wading out into the river. I suggest we follow her. Maybe she'll lead us to the Putney Lodge."

The girls waited until Lola was nearly out of sight and then followed in the car. Leaving the village, Lola struck out through the woods. Nancy parked and they continued on foot. A mile from town, near the waterfront, they saw a cabin constructed of peeled logs. An inconspicuous sign tacked to a tree read *Putney Lodge*.

"Your hunch was right, Nancy," Bess whispered as they saw Lola enter by a rear door.

Nancy hesitated. "Seeing Lola here complicates things," she said. "I'm afraid there's more to this than appears on the surface."

Just then Mrs. Putney came out on the porch. The girls remained in hiding. After she went indoors, Nancy said:

"Lola may be completely under the spell of those who have been getting money from Mrs. Putney. They may be using her services here."

"You think Lola, in a hypnotized state, is expected to steal from Mrs. Putney!" Bess gasped.

"Either that, or she may have been instructed to assist a member of the gang. I'd like to do a little scouting around before we let them know we're here."

When the girls reached town, Nancy stopped at the bank. Unfortunately it was closed for the day, but by making inquiries she located the home of the bank's president, Henry Lathrop. Nancy introduced herself and learned that her father once had brought a case to a successful conclusion for Mr. Lathrop.

"And what can I do for you?" the man inquired.

Nancy asked him if Mrs. Henry Putney had a safe-deposit box at the bank in which she might be keeping stocks, bonds, or cash.

"Her husband had a large safe-deposit box, and she has retained it."

Nancy's pulse quickened as she learned Mrs. Putney had spoken to the banker early that morning. The widow had been carrying an unusually large handbag. She had taken her box into a private room and been there some time.

"Something up?" Mr. Lathrop asked.

"I'm afraid so," Nancy answered. "I hope I'm not too late. You see, Mr. Lathrop, a gang of thieves has made away with her jewels, and I suspect that they are now after her inheritance. I've been trying to catch up with these people—"

"If what you say is true, the police should be called in to protect Mrs. Putney," the banker said.

"I agree," Nancy replied. "I have a feeling that the people who are after Mrs. Putney's money may show their hand tonight."

Later, when Nancy related her story to George and Bess, they wanted to know what she was planning.

"A call on the State Police. The next job needs strong men!"

At headquarters Nancy gave the police all the details of the case. The mob was obviously ready to strike and make a quick getaway. It was time that the law stepped in. The young detective made such an impressive presentation of the facts that she was promised that a cordon of troops would be assigned to the lake area that night.

Nancy and her friends obtained a large room at the Lake Jasper Hotel, where the police promised to notify them at once should anything develop. Nancy awoke several times during the night, wondering what might be taking place at the Putney Lodge. She had just opened her eyes again as it was beginning to grow light, when the telephone on the stand by the bed jingled.

Nancy snatched it up. She listened attentively a moment, then turned excitedly to call her friends who were still asleep.

"Girls!" she cried. "The troopers have a prisoner!"

CHAPTER XVII

Breaking a Spell

AT headquarters Nancy, Bess, and George learned that a man had been caught entering the Putney Lodge shortly after midnight. He had refused to give his name or answer any questions.

"Will you take a look at the fellow through our peephole and see if you recognize him?" the officer in charge asked. "He's in the center cell."

The three girls were led to a dark inner room. One by one they peered through a sliding wooden window which looked out upon the cell block. None of them had ever seen the prisoner in question, who was pacing the floor nervously.

"Maybe he'll break down this morning," the officer said. "Suppose you come back later."

As they left police headquarters, Nancy proposed that the girls go to the Putney cabin. When they arrived, the lodge showed signs of considerable activity. Mrs. Putney was in the living room, hurriedly packing. She made no effort to hide her displeasure at seeing the three girls.

"How did you know I was here?" she asked.

"It's a long story," Nancy replied. "But please answer one question: Do you still have your stocks and bonds safe in your handbag?"

This question evidently came as a complete surprise. The woman stammered for a moment and then sat down.

"Nancy Drew, I can't face you! You're uncanny. Not a soul in this world knew—"

"Mrs. Putney, please don't be upset," Nancy pleaded. "When you refused to take me into your confidence any longer, and left River Heights, I simply had to use my common sense as any detective would do. I'm trying to protect you against your own generous nature. You have never believed me when I told you that you are the victim of an unscrupulous gang. When I learned that you had opened your safe-deposit box I had to inform the police. It was they who caught your burglar."

The widow finally raised her head. "Yes, my securities are safe. So you—you know about the thief?"

"Very little. Tell me about him."

"It was so upsetting," the widow replied nervously. "My maid and I were sleeping soundly in our bedrooms."

So Lola was working as a maid!

"Suddenly we heard a shot fired," Mrs. Putney went on, "and there was a dreadful commotion. Several State Police officers were pounding on the door. I slipped on a dressing gown and went to see what they wanted. They asked me if I could identify the man they had caught trying to get in through a window."

"Was he anyone you knew?" asked Nancy.

"No, I never saw him before in my life. But I'm frightened. That's why I'm going home."

"And your maid?"

"I haven't told Violet yet."

Nancy quietly revealed that "Violet" was Lola White, that they had met her in the village, and were afraid she was under the influence of the same gang to which the night marauder belonged.

Mrs. Putney became more and more trusting as the conversation progressed. She was ready to admit that she had been foolish to act without advice.

"I suppose you received a spirit message to take your valuables from the bank and hold them until the spirit gave you further instructions," Nancy stated.

"Yes. My late husband contacted me."

"Will you please put them back in your safe-deposit box and not touch them again until—" Nancy hardly knew how to go on to compete with the spirit's advice—"until you have consulted Mr. Lathrop," she ended her request.

"I'll think about it," Mrs. Putney conceded. "Thank you, anyway, for all your help."

Bess spoke up, asking how Lola White happened to be working for her. Mrs. Putney said that the spirit had told her the girl would come to her at the lodge seeking employment and that she was to engage her.

"She had no luggage and told me her name was Violet Gleason," Mrs. Putney added. "She seems very nice, though odd. But if she's acting under some sort of mesmeric spell as you believe, then I don't want her around!"

"Maybe we can bring Lola out of it," Nancy suggested. "Then she'll want to go home, I'm sure. Let's go and talk to her."

Lola was sitting on the dock. As they approached her, she continued to stare at the girls without showing any sign of recognition. She was not unfriendly, however, and Nancy endeavored to bring her out of her trance by mentioning her mother, the school she had attended, a motion-picture house in River Heights, and several other familiar names. Lola merely shook her head in a bewildered way.

"Is her condition permanent?" Bess asked anxiously as the group returned to the lodge.

"I'd like to try one more thing before we take her home," Nancy said. "I don't want Mrs. White to see her this way. Mrs. Putney," she added, turning to the widow, "you will have to help us perform an experiment."

Mrs. Putney agreed to do anything to assist. However, when Nancy explained that her idea was to conduct a fake séance which would bring Lola to her senses, Mrs. Putney hesitated. Finally she said:

"I suppose it's only fair to give it a trial. And I must admit you've been right many times, Nancy. Yes, I'll help you."

While Bess and George stayed with Lola, Nancy and Mrs. Putney went to the village. The widow returned her stocks, bonds, and cash to the bank. Then they drove to Winchester, where Nancy purchased materials needed for the experiment.

At midnight the three girls posted themselves on the side porch of the lodge. Through a window they could see Mrs. Putney and Lola seated in the candle-lighted living room beside a dying log fire, as had been planned.

"Now, if only Mrs. Putney doesn't lose her nerve and give us away!" Nancy said.

"I hope we don't fumble *our* act!" Bess said, nervously adjusting her long veil and gown.

"We won't," replied Nancy. "Shall we start?"

Without showing herself, she flung wide the double doors leading from the porch into the living room. George, out of sight, waved a huge fan.

The resulting gust of wind extinguished the candles and caused the dying embers on the hearth to burst into flames.

George, hidden by darkness, reached in and uncorked a bottle of phosphorus and oil. At once a faint green light glowed spookily in the room.

Working from behind the door, Nancy, by means of a magician's reaching rod, made a large piece of cardboard appear to float in mid-air.

At the same time Bess, the long veil over her face, glided in and seated herself beside the trembling Lola. The girl half arose, then sank back, her eyes riveted on the moving cardboard.

With a quick toss of her wrist, Nancy flung it from the reaching rod, directly at Lola's feet. Plainly visible in glowing phosphorous characters was the Three Branch insigne.

Lola gasped, and even Mrs. Putney, who knew the séance was a fake, recoiled as if from a physical blow. A voice intoned:

"Lola! Lola! Give no more of your money to the orphans. They are not real, and their spirits do not need your help. Lola, do you hear me?"

There followed a moment of complete silence. Then the girl sprang to her feet, muttering:

"Yes, yes, I hear! I will obey!"

She reached out as if to grasp the arm of the figure who was veiled, and then toppled over in a faint. As Bess rejoined the other girls on the porch, Nancy closed the doors. Mrs. Putney flooded the room with light. The séance was at an end.

"Shouldn't we show ourselves now and help bring Lola out of her faint?" Bess asked anxiously as they watched through the window.

"That might give everything away," Nancy said. "I think Mrs. Putney is capable of handling things now. Let's look on from here."

To the relief of the trio, Lola soon revived.

"How are you feeling?" they heard the widow inquire solicitously.

"Sort of funny," the girl answered, rubbing her head. "Where am I?"

"At my lodge, Lola. You are employed here as a maid."

"How can that be?" the bewildered girl asked. "I work in a factory. I must get back to my job! My mother needs my help. I've been giving away too much money."

When Nancy, Bess, and George heard this, they knew the séance had been a success. Not only had Lola regained her normal thought processes, but the idea of refusing to give funds to unworthy causes also had taken firm root.

"Our work here is done," Nancy whispered to her friends. "Let's return to the hotel."

"I'm so relieved for Lola's sake," said George.

The next morning the girls decided to leave Lake Jasper without seeing Mrs. Putney again.

"I'm sure the poor woman is aware now that

she was being cheated by those people," Nancy said. "After she's had time to think matters over, she'll probably call me."

Before leaving Lake Jasper, Nancy went to the police station to see if the prisoner had revealed his identity and admitted his attempted crime.

"No, but we've sent his fingerprints to Washington to find out if he has a record," the officer said.

Nancy asked to look at him again through the peephole. This time, she felt that there was something vaguely familiar about him.

"We know by his accent he's from the South," the police officer told Nancy, "but he won't admit it, nor answer questions about his identity."

The officer turned on a tape recorder and Nancy listened to the prisoner's conversation with a guard. Only when the girls were en route home did it dawn upon Nancy that the man's voice resembled that of the New Orleans photographer!

"Girls!" she exclaimed. "Perhaps he and the prisoner are related! What was that photographer's name? Oh, yes, Towner."

Stopping at a gas station, she telephoned the police station and suggested they try out the name Towner on the prisoner, and mention New Orleans as a possible residence. In a few minutes word came back that the man had denied any connection with either one.

Nancy shrugged. "That photographer naturally

would be connected with this racket under an assumed name," she remarked.

During the drive to River Heights, the girls discussed the mystery from every angle. George and Bess were sure that the whole case soon would be solved and they praised Nancy for what she had done to prevent the gang from fleecing Mrs. Putney.

Nancy, however, pointed out that the original case involving the stolen Putney jewels still remained unsolved.

"The most valuable pieces—the pearl necklace and her husband's ring—haven't been recovered," she said. "Howard Brex, the man I suspected, hasn't been located for questioning yet. Until that has been accomplished, my work isn't done."

Upon her arrival home, pleasant news awaited Nancy. During her absence at Lake Jasper, Mr. Drew had returned.

"I've had a long trip," he remarked, a twinkle in his eye. "Traveling to New Orleans took me several hundred miles out of my way!"

Nancy's eyes opened wide. "New Orleans!" she exclaimed. "Dad, what did you learn?"

Instead of answering, the lawyer handed his daughter a small envelope.

CHAPTER XVIII

Startling Developments

NANCY opened the envelope with great excitement. Inside was a photograph of a thin-lipped, rather arrogant-looking man in his early thirties.

"Who is he?"

"Howard Brex!"

Mr. Drew explained that he had obtained the picture from the New Orleans police. Officers there still were trying to discover where he had gone since his release from prison. Nancy studied the picture and exclaimed suddenly:

"He bears a slight resemblance to the New Orleans photographer! And here's something else, Dad."

Excitedly she related the events that had taken place during his absence. In conclusion, she told about the capture of the Lake Jasper housebreaker, whose voice was very much like that of the photographer.

"Perhaps they're all related!" she speculated.

Mr. Drew offered to wire the New Orleans police for more information.

Then a telephone call confirmed the fact that Mrs. Putney had returned from Lake Jasper. Nancy hurried over to show her the photograph of Howard Brex. The widow received her graciously, but when shown the picture she insisted that she had never seen the man. Nancy had great difficulty in concealing her disappointment.

Upon returning home Nancy telephoned the Lake Jasper police for news of their prisoner. He still refused to talk, but the report from Washington on his fingerprints revealed that he had no criminal record.

No reply came to Mr. Drew's telegram, either that day or the next. But on the second day Nancy received a disturbing letter. It was signed "Mrs. Egan."

Written on cheap paper, the message was brief and threatening. It warned Nancy to give up her sleuthing activities or "suffer the consequences."

Nancy was worried. "This comes of talking to that strange woman in the park!" she thought. "But she certainly didn't look like the kind of person who would serve as a lookout for the gang."

In the hope of seeing the stranger again, Nancy watched the park most of that day. In the late afternoon she saw the woman walking rapidly toward her, carrying several packages.

Nancy stepped behind a bush until the middle-aged woman had passed. Then she followed her to a rooming house.

The woman entered an old-fashioned brick structure. Nancy waited on the stoop for a moment and then rapped on the door, which was opened by the woman she had followed. She greeted Nancy with such evident pleasure that the latter's suspicions vanished.

"Do come in. I lost the telephone number you gave me, and I've been trying for days to find out how to get in touch with you."

Nancy quickly asked a few questions to be sure she was not being misled. The woman was Mrs. Hopkins. Her daughter Nellie, she said, was at work, but should be home soon.

"After talking to you, I asked Nellie those questions you suggested!" Mrs. Hopkins revealed. "She broke down and told me everything!"

Nellie, she added, had disclosed that unknown persons frequently got in contact with her by telephone. Usually it was a woman.

"Each time this stranger called she claimed that she had received a spirit message for Nellie," Mrs. Hopkins continued. "My daughter was asked to give money to the Three Branch Home, the earthly headquarters of the spirits. Orphans are brought there and trained as mediums to carry on the work of maintaining contact with the spiritual world."

"There is no such place as Three Branch Home, Mrs. Hopkins," said Nancy. "It was just a scheme of those thieves to get money for themselves!"

"Nellie realizes that now, I think. Anyhow, she was instructed to leave her contributions on a certain day each week in the hollows of various walnut trees. The places were marked by the Three Branch sign."

"Did she do so, Mrs. Hopkins?"

"The last time Nellie went to the place, she was frightened away. She heard a sound as though someone had been struck, then she heard a moan."

Nancy was convinced that Nellie was the girl she had seen coming toward the big walnut tree where she had been struck unconscious, but she said nothing.

She continued to ask Mrs. Hopkins a few more questions. Nancy did not realize how time had flown by until a young woman, apparently returning from work, entered the room. After Nancy was introduced, Nellie Hopkins grasped the young detective's hand fervently.

"Oh, I never can thank you enough for saving me," she said gratefully. "I don't know why I let myself be taken in by those—those crooked people, except that they said good luck would come to me if I obeyed, and bad luck if I refused."

Nancy replied that she was glad to have been of

service, then she took the picture of Howard Brex from her purse. "Ever see this man?" she asked.

"You don't mean that *he* is a racketeer?" asked Nellie. "I saw him only once. He was tall and slender, and he seemed so nice," she added.

Nellie went on to say that she had met the man in the photograph when she had sat next to him on a bus. She admitted talking to him about her job and her family. She had even told him where she lived. Nellie had never seen him again, and did not even know his name, but she was sure, now, he had used her information to his own advantage. It probably was he who had turned over her address to Mrs. Egan.

Mrs. Hopkins' eyebrows raised, but she did not chide her daughter. The girl would not be so unwise again, she knew.

Nancy went home pleased to know that at last she had found a witness who could place Howard Brex with the group whose activities were connected with the disappearance of Mrs. Putney's jewels. All during the case the tall, thin man, the onetime designer of exquisite jewelry, had figured in her deductions. Just what was the part he played in the mystery? Her father, smiling broadly, opened the door.

"Time you're getting here!" he said teasingly. "I have some news."

"From New Orleans?" she asked eagerly.

"Yes, a wire came this afternoon. Your hunch

was right. The real name of that photographer you saw in New Orleans is Joe Brex. He's the brother of Howard.

"In fact, Howard has two brothers. The other one is John. Their mother was a medium in Alabama, years ago," Mr. Drew continued. "She disappeared after being exposed as a faker."

"But her sons learned her tricks!" Nancy declared. "And maybe she runs that séance place in New Orleans. Oh, Dad, thanks ever so much. We've now placed Howard and Joe Brex as members of our racketeers. I've still got to tie them up with the hocus-pocus that persuaded Mrs. Putney to bury her jewels at the designated spot, and with all of the goings-on at Blackwood Hall. But we're getting places, Dad!"

"The three brothers probably run the extortion racket together, with the woman you saw on the plane to help them," Mr. Drew said grimly.

"We must go back to Lake Jasper and talk to that prisoner tomorrow!" Nancy urged.

During the evening Mr. Drew made a call to the New Orleans police, suggesting they shadow the photographer, Joe Brex, and raid one of the services at the Church of Eternal Harmony.

Nancy's father went on to tell their suspicions concerning Joe's brothers, and to hazard the opinion that the photographer might be in league with them.

"If you can get a lead on whether Joe has been

disposing of any jewelry or other stolen articles, it might be the breaking point in our case."

"We'll see what information we can get for you," the officer told Mr. Drew.

"While I think of it," the lawyer finished, "if you can locate a picture of John Brex, will you send it to me at once?"

"Glad to do it," the officer replied.

The next morning, while Nancy was packing a change of clothes in case she and her father should stay overnight at Lake Jasper, Hannah Gruen brought in a telegram to Mr. Drew. Since he received many such messages, his daughter thought little about this one until she heard him utter an exclamation of surprise in the next room. Running to him, she asked what the wire said.

"Joe Brex recently left New Orleans in a hurry! His whereabouts is not known. The Church of Eternal Harmony was found locked, and the medium gone. The police couldn't locate a picture of John Brex, they say."

Before Nancy could comment, Hannah summoned her to the telephone. "Lake Jasper police calling."

The officer on the wire was brief. "Miss Drew, I'd like your help," he said. "That prisoner who wouldn't talk broke jail last night under very mysterious circumstances! The guard says there was a ghost in his cell!"

CHAPTER XIX

Trapped!

THE story that the Lake Jasper police told Nancy was a startling one.

On the previous night, the cell block had been guarded by an easygoing, elderly man who served as relief during the late hours of the night.

According to his story, he had been making a routine check tour of the cell block, when suddenly a pale-green, ghostly figure appeared to be flitting through the air inside the center cell. A sepulchral voice called him by name and said: "I am the spirit of your dear wife Hattie. Is all well with you? If you will unlock the cell, and come in where I am waiting to speak to you, I will tell you about our Johnny who was drowned and of Allan who was killed in the war."

In fear and trembling, the guard had obeyed. No sooner had he entered the cell when a damp cloth was pressed against his nostrils, and his keys seized from his belt. Just before he lost consciousness he heard the cell door clang shut.

"The same old trick!" exclaimed Nancy.

She told the officer on the telephone the latest information Mr. Drew had received, and their conclusion that the three Brex brothers were responsible for the spirit racket.

"We think your prisoner was John Brex. One of his confederates must have supplied him with the information about the guard. But how could anyone get inside the jail to deliver the spirit paraphernalia to the man in the cell?" asked Nancy.

"Well, a woman came to the office and told us that she understood we were holding an unidentified burglar. She asked if she might visit the prisoner. One of our men took her to the cell and stayed with her in the corridor."

"Was the guard with her all the time she was inside the cell block?" Nancy asked.

"Yes, he was," the officer at the other end of the telephone replied. "Wait a minute," he added quickly. "He left her when she fainted."

"Fainted?" repeated Nancy.

"Well, the woman looked at the prisoner for a long time without a word. Then suddenly she fell to the floor. Our man ran to get some spirits of ammonia. When he got back she was still out, but came around in a jiffy when he applied the smelling salts to her nose."

"There's your answer," said Nancy. "She was a

member of the Brex setup and passed the robe and other things through the bars while the guard was out of the corridor. Where is she now?"

"Gone," replied the officer. "When we took her back to the office she told us that she had thought the man in the cell was her brother she hadn't seen in fifteen years, but decided he wasn't. We had to let her go."

"Well, I think when you catch up with Brex and his fainting visitor you will find them to be confederates," Nancy said.

The officer thanked Nancy for the explanation, and said a nation-wide alarm would be sent out on the escaped prisoner.

"Wherever those gangsters are, I'm sure they didn't have time to take all their loot with them," Nancy remarked to Ned the next afternoon as they sat together in his car in front of the Drew home. "They must have hidden it somewhere around here. Let's try to think where they would be most apt to cache it until things blow over and it becomes safe for them to collect it."

"Some bank vault?" Ned suggested.

"I doubt it. My hunch would be Blackwood Hall."

"But the troopers searched the place."

Nancy reminded him that although the police had been skeptical about her story, she was sure a live "ghost" had come out of one wall and gone through another in the old mansion.

"And those creaking sounds—" Suddenly she snapped her fingers. "There must be some way of getting from the underground room to the upstairs floors without using the stairs."

"Gosh, you could be right! How about hidden stairs between the walls?" Ned asked.

"I'm more inclined to think it may be a secret elevator—one you can operate by pulling ropes to raise and lower it," said Nancy.

"Let's go!" said Ned.

"Wait just a minute while I run into the house. I want to tell Hannah where we're going."

Nancy returned in a moment, and they set out for Blackwood Hall.

"So much about the place hasn't been explained," Nancy said thoughtfully. "Those sliding panels, for instance. They may be entrances to secret rooms as well as to an old elevator!"

In case they should run into trouble, Ned stopped at home and got his short-wave radio sending set.

When they reached Blackwood Hall, Nancy suggested that they separate, and he keep watch outside, in case any of the racketeers should show up. Ned agreed to the plan.

"Yell if you find anything, and I'll come running," he declared.

Nancy took a small tool kit from the car. Once in the house, working inch by inch, she made an inspection by flashlight of the second- and third-floor hallways of the dwelling. There was no evidence of any spring or contrivance that could move the carved walnut panels.

"The panel on the third floor must open from the outside," Nancy said aloud, "for I distinctly saw the "ghost" emerge from the wall on the second floor and disappear *into* the wall in the third-floor hallway. I'll have a look at the basement room and then come back here with a hatchet."

The main part of the basement, entered from the kitchen, revealed nothing to indicate the existence of a hidden elevator.

"If there is one, it must be in that secret room after all," Nancy decided.

Using the hidden door in the organ room, she slowly descended the steps. Her flashlight cut a circular pattern on the cracked walls of the tunnel as she played the light from side to side.

Finally Nancy reached the walnut door. To her amazement it now was bolted on the inner side, but with the tools from the car she managed to let herself in.

All was quiet inside the pitch-dark room. From the doorway, Nancy played her flashlight quickly around the four sides of the room. Satisfied that it was empty, she entered cautiously.

The door behind her creaked softly. Nancy

whirled around. There was no draft, yet the heavy walnut door seemed to move several inches. The door must be improperly hung, she thought.

Then, inch by inch, she began to inspect the paneled walls. At the far end of the room, she came upon a section which she found, upon minute examination, was not in a true line with the rest of the woodwork.

"This may be something!" Nancy thought, her pulse pounding.

She tugged and pushed at the paneling. Suddenly it began to move. It slid back all the way to reveal, just as Nancy had expected, a small, old-fashioned elevator, consisting of a wooden platform suspended on ropes, with another rope extending through a hole in the floor.

But her first thrill of discovery gave way to a cry of horror. Facing her in the elevator were two men—Howard Brex and his brother John, the escaped prisoner from Lake Jasper!

Confronted by the pair, Nancy backed away and tried to flee through the walnut doorway. Howard Brex seized her arm while the other man, holding a flashlight, blocked the exit.

"No, you don't!" Howard warned. "You've made enough trouble for us."

"I'm not afraid of you or your brother!" Nancy stated defiantly. "The police will be here any minute."

"Yes?" the man mocked. "If you're depending

"Nancy Drew, you've made enough trouble!" Howard
Brex rasped

on your boy friend to rescue you, guess again. We'll take care of him as soon as we dispose of you."

Nancy was dismayed to hear that the man knew Ned was awaiting her outside. She realized that if she screamed for help, it would only draw him into the trap.

"What do you plan to do with me?" she demanded.

"We'll take care of you, so you'll never bother us again," Howard Brex replied as he shoved her roughly toward the elevator. "Fact is, we've decided, since you have such a fondness for ghosts, to let you spend the remainder of your life with the ghost of Blackwood Hall!"

"You had plenty of warning," Howard went on. "But would you mind your own business? No! Not even after I knocked you out in the woods one day when you were spying on one of my clients."

Nancy knew she must keep them talking. As soon as Ned became concerned about her long absence he would radio for help. "So you admit you've cheated innocent people with your fake séances," she remarked.

"Sure, and don't think it isn't a good racket!" John Brex boasted.

"How many people have you fleeced?"

"So many that we'll be able to take a long vacation," his brother bragged.

"You sold some of Mrs. Putney's jewelry. But you still have her most valuable pieces!" Nancy accused him.

"Sure," Howard agreed. "We'll wait until the hubbub dies down. We'll sell the necklace and her husband's ring after we skip the country."

"You climbed along the roof outside of Mrs. Putney's bedroom window at night and spoke to her as if you were her husband's spirit," Nancy went on accusingly.

"You're a smart kid," John Brex mocked.

"You do know a lot," said Howard. "Even more than I thought. Well, the sooner we get this job over with, John, the better for us."

"I suppose your mother helped with the racket," Nancy remarked, hoping to gain time. "She ran those fake séances in New Orleans, and pretended to be the portrait of Amurah coming to life."

"It was a good trick," Howard said boastfully.

"She had a double wall built in the house so she could hide there?" Nancy asked.

"Sure, and she did the rapping back there, too."

"Was the old man at the Church of Eternal Harmony your brother Joe?"

"Yes, in disguise. The whole family's in the racket. John's wife has been helping us, and her friend, too."

"The friend is the one who drives the car, isn't she?" Nancy queried.

"Wouldn't you like to know?" John sneered.

"And she hypnotizes people?"

"No!" growled Howard. "She just gives them a whiff that makes them drowsy. *I* do the hypnotizing. Whenever any of my clients get out of line, I produce the beckoning hand."

"One of your luminous wax hands," declared Nancy. "And you must be a ventriloquist as well. Lola White nearly lost her life walking into the river because you hypnotized her," she accused him.

"That was your fault," the man replied. "You came snooping around here before I had a chance to get her out of it."

"Did you do your hypnotizing near the walnut trees that were used as hiding places for money and letters?" Nancy asked. "Or at the cabin where you held the fake séances?"

"Both places."

"I imagine the Three Branch symbol represented you three clever brothers."

"That'll be enough from you, young lady," snarled John. "I'm getting fed up with this dame's wisecracks, Howie!"

"You even played the organ," Nancy said coolly, turning to Howard. "And when you didn't have to use the dummy ghost, you dressed like one yourself."

John interrupted roughly, "This has gone far enough."

Before Nancy could ask another question, the men thrust her into the elevator. Her flashlight and car tools were taken from her.

"Nancy Drew, you're about to take your last ride!" Howard told her brutally. "In a few moments, young lady, you will join the ghost of Blackwood Hall!"

CHAPTER XX

A Hidden Discovery

THE secret panel closed in Nancy's face. A few moments later she felt the rope beside her moving and the lift began to rise slowly upward with a creaking, groaning sound.

What were John and Howard Brex going to do now? Move out their loot? Capture Ned?

With a jerk, the elevator suddenly halted. Nancy tugged at the rope. It would not move!

At the same moment, Nancy saw a faint, greenish glow arising from one corner of her prison. Presently she became aware of an unpleasant odor rapidly growing stronger. Then Nancy understood.

"Those fiends uncorked a bottle of phosphorus and oil in this elevator, and they've probably added a deadly sleeping potion for me to inhale," she thought, breaking out in cold perspiration. "That's what they meant by saying that in a few moments I would join the ghost of Blackwood Hall. They meant Jonathan Humphrey, who died in the duel. I'll die at Blackwood Hall too!"

For an instant Nancy nearly gave way to panic. Then reason reasserted itself.

From her pocket she took a handkerchief. Covering her nose and mouth with it, she groped about frantically on the floor of the dark elevator. Guided by the greenish glow, she found a small bottle in one corner.

Already weak and dizzy, Nancy had no time to search further for the stopper. Instead, she pulled off her suit jacket and jammed part of the sleeve into the opening of the bottle.

Immediately the light was extinguished. But Nancy by now felt so drowsy that she was forced to sit down.

Sleep overcame her. She had no idea of how much later it was when she awoke. But now she felt stronger. The sickening odor was gone. She could think clearly.

She pounded against the wooden sides of the elevator shaft. Three of the walls seemed to be as solid as stone. Only the fourth seemed thin. Could this be the panel of the third-floor hallway?

The old house was as still as death itself. Nancy was certain Howard and John Brex had fled, and no doubt they had captured Ned too. As time dragged on and still no one came, she became convinced that her friend had met with disaster.

"I told Hannah that Ned and I were coming here," Nancy thought. "She'll be worried about our long absence and send help."

Then a harrowing thought came to her. Maybe her friends had come and gone while she was asleep! By the luminous hands of her wrist watch, Nancy knew she had been in the elevator over two hours

"It's no use!" she despaired. Then instantly she added, "I *mustn't* give up hope!"

Nancy sat down again on the floor, trying to figure out some means of escape. But scarcely had she closed her eyes to concentrate than she became aware of sounds.

Pressing an ear against the crack between the elevator floor and the wall, Nancy listened intently. With a thrill of joy she recognized Bess's high-pitched voice. Then she heard others speaking: her father, Hannah Gruen, and George Fayne.

Nancy began to shout and pound on the elevator door. Attracted by the noise, her friends came running up the stairway. Nancy kept shouting directions, until finally they were able to locate the wall panel behind which she was imprisoned.

"Nancy!" her father called. "Are you all right?"

"Yes, Dad, but I'm in an elevator and can't get out. I can't even move it."

"We'll soon find a way. If we can't open this panel, we'll tear the wall down!"

"Is Ned safe?" Nancy asked anxiously.

"Haven't seen him," her father replied. "Hannah got worried after you'd been gone so long, and told us you had come here. Ned isn't with you?"

"No," Nancy replied in a discouraged voice, then added, "Please go down to the ghost room and see if you can find out how to move this elevator."

Several minutes passed, then Mr. Drew reported no success.

"It's a very old-fashioned hand type and works by pulling a rope," he said. "Evidently they have locked the wheel over which the rope passes at the top. Well, here goes the wall!"

Nancy heard a thud, then the sound of splintering wood. A moment later light beamed through a small hole.

"Hand me the flashlight," said Nancy. "Maybe I can find out how the panel opens."

In a few moments Nancy located a lock. Releasing it, she pushed up the section of wall and tumbled into her father's arms.

"Thank goodness you're safe!" Hannah cried, hugging her in turn. "When you didn't come home, I knew something had happened!"

"Bless you, Hannah, for bringing help!" Nancy exclaimed.

From the yard came the sharp yipping of a dog. "Why, that sounds like Togo!" Nancy exclaimed.

"We left him in the car," her father explained. "Something must have excited him."

Hastening downstairs, the party reached the front porch just as several state troopers, surrounding two women and two men, emerged from the woods. Nancy was overjoyed to see Ned leading the procession!

"They've captured Howard and John Brex!" she cried. "And that first woman with them—she's the one we met on the plane. The other must be the veiled chauffeur!"

Ned ran to Nancy's side. Breathlessly he explained that upon seeing the two men leaving Blackwood Hall, he had hurriedly summoned state troopers by means of the short-wave set.

"Then I trailed the Brex brothers and kept sending my location to the police. What a chase!"

"You did a swell job, fellow," complimented one of the troopers. "We sure had a hard time trying to keep up with you."

"We caught the men and the women at a little hotel down the river," Ned added. "They were packing their duds, intending to make a getaway."

"Good work, Ned!" Nancy congratulated him. "This practically winds up the case, except for capturing Joe Brex."

"Don't worry about that," Mr. Drew interposed. "The police will run him in before forty-eight hours have elapsed."

The four prisoners refused to talk when confronted by Nancy and her party. Though they would not admit that they had any loot hidden at Blackwood Hall or elsewhere, their arrogance was completely gone. Howard Brex looked completely crestfallen when Nancy repeated to the troopers all the damaging evidence he had boastfully revealed to her a few hours earlier.

When Ned heard how they had put her in the elevator to die, he was filled with remorse. Having no idea anything more had happened than Nancy had smoked out the gangsters, he had felt it all right to leave her and go after them.

"I'll never do that again!" he vowed.

Tearfully, John Brex's wife, the woman they had seen on the plane, admitted her identity. She acknowledged having trailed the three girls to New Orleans after learning that Mrs. Putney had engaged Nancy to find the stolen jewelry. When they threw her off the scent, and she saw them coming out of the Church of Eternal Harmony and heading for the photographer's, she hastened to warn Joe. John happened to be there, and the three concocted the scheme of putting the warning on the plate and carrying Nancy away in a car to an empty house in order to frighten her off the case.

Mrs. Brex's friend also admitted her guilt. She had adopted clever disguises for the sole purpose of deceiving Nancy, as well as the people the group sought to cheat. It was she who had picked up the Egan letters at the hotel.

"Don't say another word!" John shouted. "You've said too much already!"

Here George interrupted to address Howard Brex. "After you had abandoned having séances at Blackwood Hall and moved your equipment by wheelbarrow to the cabin, we tracked you there and found smoke—acrid smoke, not wood smoke, coming out the chimney and from under the door."

Howard sneered. "Had you guessing, eh? All I was doing was trying out a new brand of spirit powder. I ducked out a back window when I heard someone trying to break into the place."

After the prisoners were taken off to jail, Nancy suggested that a trooper remain at Blackwood Hall with her and the others to investigate the paneled walls of the rambling old house.

"I want you all to take an elevator ride with me!" Nancy said gaily, "and see if we can locate the gangsters' loot."

The wall panel on the third floor still stood open. Nancy swung a flashlight around the elevator. In a moment she found what she was looking for: the mechanism to run the car. It was high up in the shaft under the roof. An iron bar was thrust through the wooden wheel over which the rope ran.

In a moment the wheel again was free. Using the rope, Nancy lowered the elevator platform to the level of the second floor. There she examined carefully each wall of the elevator shaft. To her joy she located the spring that operated the panel from the inside. It rolled back exposing the second-floor hall.

Then she turned her attention to the opposite wall of the elevator shaft. It, too, seemed to be a panel, and she went over every inch of it for a catch. When she found it, she pressed the release and the panel slid noiselessly upward.

"A secret room!" she cried.

The others crowded around her. Before them stood a manikin dressed in flimsy white, as well as reaching rods, bottles of phosphorus, oil, and several books on hypnotism.

Besides these, the searchers found box upon box of envelopes stuffed with bills. But most important was a notebook containing the names and addresses of people who had been swindled by the spirit racket.

"This money will help repay all those people who have been robbed," Nancy declared.

Under the eaves Nancy came upon a large chest which proved to contain a complete set of craftsmen's tools such as a jeweler would use—Howard Brex's outfit.

"I suppose those clever imitations which Mr. Freeman detected when Mrs. Putney took them to

be cleaned were fashioned right here in Blackwood Hall," Mr. Drew said thoughtfully.

"But where are Mrs. Putney's missing gems?"
Nancy asked.

"Right here in this envelope!" George spoke
up. "Now your work on the case is really complete." Turning to the officer, she said, "Nancy
got into this thing trying to trace Mrs. Putney's
stolen jewelry. Whoever would have thought that
all this could happen before the thieves were
caught?"

The following day, events occurred very rapidly. Joe Brex and his mother were arrested in
Chicago. Joe acknowledged he had built up a
good business in spirit photography.

He and the others finally confessed their full
part in the sordid Three Branch swindle, and admitted that they first cajoled, then threatened
their victims when they did not yield to the
suggestions of the spirits. The men also admitted
having stolen Mr. Drew's car to move out some of
their props.

To celebrate the successful conclusion of the
mystery, Hannah Gruen planned a surprise dinner and invited all of Nancy's closest friends, and
also Mrs. Putney.

"Oh, my dear," the widow said, tears in her
eyes, "I was so unfair to you in my thoughts. At
times I felt you lacked all understanding of my
case. But you've made me realize how utterly stu-

pid I was to be fooled into thinking my husband's spirit was giving me messages. Now, dear, I know you won't accept money as a reward for the work you have done in my behalf, but I hope you will take as an expression of my everlasting gratitude this cameo ring which belonged to my husband's mother. It is one of the jewels you helped me to recover."

"Oh, Mrs. Putney, I couldn't," protested Nancy.

"Nonsense," Mrs. Putney interrupted. "I have no one to inherit my lovely things when I go. I want you to have it as a memento of a case you solved in which many innocent people were saved from serious loss."

"You are very generous, Mrs. Putney. I would love to wear it. I enjoyed every moment I was working on the mystery—except the quagmire and the elevator incident," Nancy declared. "Dad," she said, turning to Mr. Drew, "I would never have done it without all the help you gave me."

"Ridiculous," Mr. Drew objected.

"I'll bet you could tackle your next case single-handed," Mrs. Putney insisted.

That exciting mystery, *The Clue of the Leaning Chimney*, was to come as a baffling surprise to the girl detective.

"Say," said George, laughing, "we learned enough about magicians' tricks to go into the ghost business ourselves. How about fitting up a studio at Blackwood Hall and running séances?"

Bess shivered. "No, thanks. We've just learned that it never pays to flimflam the public."

"Anyway, it's much more fun to catch the people who try to do the flimflamming!" Nancy said, smiling.

Match Wits with The Hardy Boys®!

Collect the Complete
Hardy Boys Mystery Stories®
by Franklin W. Dixon

The Hardy Boys Back-to-Back
#1: The Tower Treasure/#2: The House on the Cliff

Celebrate over 70 Years with the World's Greatest Super Sleuths!

Match Wits with Super Sleuth Nancy Drew!

Collect the Complete
Nancy Drew Mystery Stories®
by Carolyn Keene

Nancy Drew Back-to-Back

Celebrate over 70 years with the World's Best Detective!